Passages

A Trilogy:
Book Three:
The Circle Ends

Sandra Waine

Solstice Publishing - www.solsticepublishing.com

Passages Book Three

The Circle Ends

Sandra Waine

Dedication:

To all my family and friends. Especially those that know I
am a bit nuts but appreciate me just exactly as I am.
Thank you.

Chapter One

Where was the light? His arms moved about, feeling the rough sand against his hands. Where the hell was Sam? An old face he did not recognize placed a foul-smelling concoction under his nose, speaking in Arabic. Fuck, this was not what he had expected. Through hazed vision, he could see he was still in the Middle East.

Damn, he thought. He had not left the country.

Had she?

Ears perked, Adam listened as background noises were identified. Women with hushed voices were coming closer to him, along with the sound of shuffling feet. Off in the distance he could hear the flap of a tent billowing in the hot desert wind.

Then someone yelled. It was a faintly recognizable voice. But Adam just did not have enough mental strength right now to figure out who the heck it was.

"Come, girl! Get over here now with that stronger potion. I need to get him up and onto his feet before anyone comes snooping around. I can't lift him alone. He's too tall and muscular. Damn it, girl, has your head stopped working? Hand me that. Quickly now. We must get him hidden!"

Something more obnoxiously rancid than the last concoction was placed under his nose just as he inhaled a deep breath. Rapidly, his head turned away from it, eyes flashing open to glare into the dark orbs of an Egyptian woman. Dressed in ancient robes, she leaned closer, clutching a hand-carved walking stick. As his focus cleared and eyesight returned, he glanced at the circle of women surrounding them, a grin starting to form.

Well, if he had died this was not too bad, he

thought. They were all mighty attractive. Ironically, it appeared he held more interest to them than the small group of old men hovering off in the distance. Relief spread through his body. None were carrying any weapons.

"Who are you?"

"Do you really not know me? Honestly? Take a closer look at my face."

Recognition dawned bright as he maneuvered and stood. Quickly, he took her rather roughly by the arm, eyes boring into hers. "Alwen? Is that you?"

"That took you long enough. Now move along and come with me. We need to get you inside a tent before any of the common traders come by on their route to the palace. I'm not prepared to lie for you just yet. As to why you are here and who you are."

He moved about, stunned, yet fully aware now of this new environment. "Is Samantha here?"

"Absolutely. Where is not clear. Although I can confirm she is definitely not in this encampment."

"Shit. I think I screwed things up. I followed her. This is not good. I am damned and will not be able to return unless circumstances are changed. Someone will need to intervene for me. Is that you? This is no time for secrecy. I must know what the hell is going on. All of it."

"Now calm down. You are getting way ahead of yourself. Right now you need to step back. Take a deep breath and try to relax. Do you feel different? Is this all new to you? It is for me. That I can assure you. I believe it may be for many of us that are locked in this circle with your Samantha. So, consider this. It could be right this time, Adam. We have no choice but to go with it."

He raised a skin-roughened hand over his face and through thick hair. "Okay. Give me all the details you can."

"That a new addition would be arriving with her, but not that it was you specifically. I'm here to help two transients. Now that part fits together. Regardless, I am fully prepared to take you where you need to be."

"That was a bit much to follow, but I think I get it. Just where is my next destination? Why can't I remember everything? I know I came through the passage with her, but things are hazy. I don't know why I am here. I've never had so little control."

"There is another woman who is expecting you. We will remain here until nightfall. Then move under darkness to her location." Stopping suddenly, she turned abruptly around, as if she knew what was maneuvering around in that mind of his.

"I see that expression in your eyes. Don't get it in your mind it's her. It is not."

"I don't suppose you have any idea who she is and what she wants with me? This other woman?"

He sat down on a plush cushion as a plate of food and a brass jug filled with wine was set before him. He smiled up into the comely lass's pretty face. One eyebrow shot up as he noticed Alwen's disapproving glance over a fully robed shoulder.

"No, I think you already know the answer to that. When the time is appropriate, you will be made aware."

His gaze lowered, evaluating this new attire. Or rather, old attire from centuries ago. "What is the meaning of this bar and chain I wear? I know I've seen it before. But, can't say when."

"Oh, yes. You are going to want to conceal that. I nearly forgot to tell you. I have a different robe for you to put on. Problem is I can't hide your sandals. We have no replacements for you here."

"Woman, you have been speaking nothing but gibberish!"

They were both getting agitated.

"You can't remember yet, I know. Your contact tonight will enlighten you more than I can provide. That is not the reason I am here. It's only to keep the grass from

growing beneath your feet, so to speak. And perhaps—"
She glanced at the young, pretty girl eyeing him. "—to
keep you out of mischief."

Slugging back a large gulp of the pungent dark red
wine, he shook his head in frustration. It was true. His
memory was only providing bits and pieces of his life here.
Why? he internally wondered, trying in vain to find the key
to answers burning in his mind. But they would not come.
The key was hidden from him this time.

Alwen watched the emotional upheaval wash over
his features. "Adam, this is good. You are not quite sure of
things. This is indeed a good sign."

She nodded toward the girl, signaling her exit. "Go
easy on that. It is important to remember every word
spoken to you this evening and after that. I can tell you feel
strange. But take my last words of advice. Let everything
and everyone flow as they must. Do not get in the way."

"Fair enough to it all. I can already feel my insides
on fire from this potent drink."

She rose, preparing to leave, but then turned,
clutching both flaps. "You are known as a philanderer here,
my friend. Take care with whom you dally. Let it not be
any of the handsome girls. Be warned."

He grinned as she shrugged and let the flaps fall
into place. Her voice, loud and commanding, could be
heard while walking away. "Girls, girls, come along. We
need to gather wood and get those sheep tended. I don't see
the water jugs filled yet!"

He laughed, listening to the tirade. How long was
she here? Probably only until tonight and then would
disappear back to Baglen. Leaning back on the cushions, he
rested his head on his hand as eyes drifted closed. His mind
wandered back to their last few days in Luxor. Only bits
and pieces came back. But one part he recalled with clarity.
Their lovemaking.

He opened them back up and stared at the pitch in

the tent top. "Why" he mouthed softly, "are you trying to vanquish thoughts of Sam from my mind? Already the curve of her small waist is disappearing from my sight. Would you have me take another while I am here? Is she already engulfed with someone? I now forgotten?"

Adam listened intently but there was complete silence.

No one was going to answer his question.

Darkness descended as he finally gave in to the potent wine and drifted off. When he woke, a plate of smoked meats and more of the wine he now had to be careful with had been placed on a mat next to him. Suddenly he was hungry. Grabbing a few juicy pieces, he chewed rapidly while reaching for fresh figs and grapes. The noise level outside was gaining momentum as it got closer and closer to his tent. Taking one final swig of the wine, he set the goblet down, not wanting a repeat of a few hours earlier.

One of the tent flaps slid open and Alwen stood just inside, hands raised resting on wide, maidenly hips, just as he'd seen her do a dozen times back in Shropshire. Funny, he thought, he could recall more about Alwen than Sam right now.

"Gather yourself up. The time is ripe and we are ready to go. Come along."

Once outside the tent, it took a few seconds for his eyes to adjust. It had been a very long time since he had been engulfed in such total darkness as this. Out in the desert with only the stars and a quarter moon, they set out on foot as a very small band. Two men, Alwen and Adam.

High up in the sky, the constellation of Orion was their guide as he followed them along in silence. Adam had read about this cluster. In fact, the journal of a famous explorer's recount of how it had aided in their group's direction when they thought they were lost in the desert, forever still fascinated him.

The recount claimed that it was the same exact distance as the Giza pyramid complex. Depending on which theory you wanted to believe, it was said that the full Milky Way correlated along with other pyramids and the Nile. If that indeed was the case, then he was south of Cairo by quite a distance. Or rather, Memphis, which he recalled was the old name before it was changed in later centuries.

Frivolous information like this kept his mind engaged as they trekked on. It also allowed thoughts of her from creeping back in. They walked on for several more hours before distant speckles of light finally flickered on the dark horizon. Yet it was still the middle of the night.

Alwen motioned him up to the front as the two men stood opposite, preparing to head on in a different direction. She nodded to them both in thanks, taking Adam by the arm. "We will now go to her cave. It's a short distance. Then I will leave, my task completed. Just a bit more advice for you that was requested I pass along. With her, you are not to ask any questions. She is, as they say, gifted. Therefore, a bit peculiar, if you know what I mean. Just pay attention. Listen. Watch. Especially her facial expressions. There is much to be learned by this visit."

"Okay."

As they neared, his eyes were drawn toward the outline of a series of famous porphyritic caves. Even in this era, they were considered quite a natural phenomenon. Centuries later, archaeologists and geologists alike would find many hidden treasures that would shed light on the type of people that dwelled in them, thrived and survived.

The torch lights grew in intensity as he noticed a few men cloaked in robes, hoods pulled up, stationed at various locations for protection. The goat path they climbed was narrow and rocky, making it tricky for him to keep his footing while attempting to absorb the area.

At the largest cave they paused. Adam accidently bumped into Alwen's plump form. Reaching out just in time and clasping an arm, he prevented her from tumbling down to the dirt.

Smiling, she silently motioned him ahead.

Pausing and turning slightly to thank her, Adam met with thin air. She had already disappeared to God knew where. He hoped it was back to Baglen.

"Enter." A strong female voice beckoned him further as the light flickering off the walls gave a clear depiction of the hieroglyphics. A great battle was taking place. Halting, he stared at it, totally engrossed. Someone, somewhere, from another time, had once said it was both bloody and beautiful. He racked his brain, trying to recall who that was and where he had seen this before.

"Prince Jared Malik, come and sit with me. You will not be spending that much time here. So, I now require your full attention."

He sat opposite the woman, trying to decipher her dark facial features from the poor lighting inside the cave. "I am listening. Go on."

"Your people need you from a distant land. They are expecting your return to them shortly. Are you aware of what has brought you here? Whom? Why?"

His brain started to work again. Prince. Did she say prince? He readjusted on the beautifully woven eastern rug, its roughness scratching his legs where they were not covered by the robe.

"You do not remember, do you?"

"No. Nothing yet. What am I to see?"

"Many things. Here, take this orb and hold it with both your hands. Now sit still, relax and glance into it. Tell me what comes into your vision."

It was cold to the touch as he cupped it. Both eyes suddenly started to blur. He blinked rapidly for several seconds, before at last images flashed into play. "A beautiful woman. I am drawn to her. But she's dressed differently. She's not a Hyskos. I think her name is Sam. I see a burning village and a bloody, fierce battle. Has this happened already or is this something that will happen again?"

The woman did not answer the question about the battle. "Here she is not spoken of by that name. Caution yourself not to use it. She is referred to as Nofret Qalhata, the beautiful one of ancient Egypt. She is a healer. Highly esteemed in her village, the valleys and with the queen."

"Go on."

"You will be taken to your village shortly, where all your memory will return once you drink the wine. Do not be concerned it is poison. Do not fight your destiny again, Prince Malik. May my warning be clear. This is the final time. If you both do not correct the past changes in history, it will never be right for the rest of us. This circle will continue. The very last time you sat here and we spoke, about her and all that has occurred, you did not keep your word. You must this time. She needs your strength."

This time? Last time? His mind bolted into a frenzy of thoughts.

"What did I do wrong? I can't remember. You have to guide me better than this if we are to succeed."

"I cannot. It is against the order. But mark on this day my words. Keep them circling around inside your head. Especially when you see her again and your heart has different ideas. A whole gathering of people anxiously awaits a different outcome. An event of great magnitude is coming again. This time you need to get it done. At all costs."

A cold, penetrating shiver passed through him. What had he fucked up previously? Damn. He was frustrated, lifting a hand up to run it through his hair. Then it stopped as it met with a turban.

"You can remove that once you are in your tent. You will not need it after that."

He stared down at the orb again, seeing additional

details. Flashes of her. Leaning over him. But why were they not kissing? Prince Malik knew the reason.

It was Rano blocking the way.

He stood tall and arrogant in his chariot, sword drawn, strong hands holding the reins and keeping the horses at bay. Then Prince Malik saw and heard a scream. Yes, it was a piercing, wrenching scream followed by the low chant of distraught women.

Something of great sadness had occurred. Then the prayers followed. He tried to look away but could not. Was he dead? Some members of other villages were being herded onto barges and moved. Although they were not family, he knew them from trading and recognized clearly the weaving on their blankets. They were Hebrews.

A stronger force lifted his face to the woman's as he reached out, handing the orb over.

"Ah, yes. Now you are truly beginning to see more clearly."

"Yes. Enough. I know what will happen when I get to the village. I am now prepared."

She nodded, handing him bread, ground olives and chickpeas. He scooped it up and gulped down wine from a rawhide flask.

"What do you need to remember this time that you have ignored all other times? This is important."

"I will listen. Give her room. Be open when words of great revelation come my way."

"You understand the gravity of this all? This time?"

"Yes. Fully."

"Good. You will go now. There are men waiting who will take you by horseback to the village. They are your people."

"Can I ask your name?"

"Can you not see me clear enough to know?" She raised a torch and kept it to the left of her face, showering it with strong light.

His jaw dropped. "Gerda? You? Do you go by that name here?"

She laughed softly. "No, it's hardly Egyptian or even Hebrew. But that matters little, for I leave soon. If I should see you again, back in our correct century and all seems as it was, then you were not successful." She rose, placing the torch back on the roped loop. Then she walked back into the darkness of the cave, disappearing from his view completely.

"But wait. Don't you mean if I do not see you again...?" He took a few steps toward her, but already knew it was futile. She was long on her way to somewhere else.

Walking outside to the waiting men, he glanced off into the horizon and wondered how the hell this time he would make Nofret realize what she needed to do. Could he keep his word? He kicked a stone and watched as it launched over the trail down into a rocky ravine.

His mind went silent. No one was going to give him any help here.

One thing was very clear: what Gerda said and how she said it. There was no mistaking the gravity of it all. Thankful for the interruption, he turned toward one of the men.

"Your horse, Prince Malik. We must ride hard and fast to arrive in the village before the sun brightens the day."

He mounted and they rode at breakneck speed through the darkness, the moon and stars above providing a soft light. As the sun was breaking the horizon with its beautifully colorful display, they arrived at his village. He jumped down, handing the reins over, and entered what he knew instantly was his own tent.

Immediately his eyes scanned over a battle tunic, shield, knife, and a menacing, deadly spear. He knew these weapons well.

"Brother, why do you ride out into the very desert we prepare to battle the Pharaoh's army on this day?"

He turned and clasped both of the man's hands with his own. "I needed a visit with the crone, Gerda, my brother Ahmall. I wanted to see if their camp lights shined from high above. But they were only a distant flicker. There will be no full moon to guide tonight. The men are ready?"

"Yes, and the women have all gone to the caves under the protection of a few of our Hebrew brothers. I saw to that myself in your absence."

"Excellent. Come. Sit. Let us break bread and drink. Then we will prepare for battle."

They sat talking as his mind wandered, recalling Gerda's words earlier this day about seeing more after drinking the wine. He took a full cup, finished, then waited.

It happened in a quick succession of visions. His tribal brother had risen to get another jug and did not notice how distant his prince had become.

Ahmall reached over, taking his arm. "Should we meet our maker this day, know that I love you. You are a fierce warrior and welcoming friend. I have no doubt we will meet again in another lifetime."

Oh, Prince Malik thought quickly, silently, *if only he knew how true that could be*. Now he knew who this was: Sam's brother. But apparently, Ahmall had no recollection of either of them into the future. This, Prince Malik found very strange, as the air inside the tent suddenly crackled with an unknown force.

Both men turned in fascination as a cold breeze flew through, lifting the tent flaps for a few seconds, then dispersed without a trace.

"What the hell was that? It's hotter than hell outside right now. The noonday sun is not even high in the sky yet."

"I have no idea, Malik. Never seen anything like it. Do you think we are cursed? That it was the cold winds of death coming now to mark our souls?"

Ahmall was clearly spooked, but Prince Malik shook it off. "I can't explain that. But we will not bow down to such a force as that. Will we? Our people deserve a chance. If we cower before even reaching the battle, what kind of men are we?"

That brought him around.

Ahmall stood. "God will not see the destruction of good people this day at the hands of those that would diminish our worth. We are a powerful nation. More powerful than their enemies in the east and south. We will win in the end, brother. I know it."

Prince Malik had to wonder if he was referring to thousands of years down the road of time. "It is no longer in our hands. Now, go and prepare yourself. We must ready as the camp rises." Ahmall thumped his chest with an iron fist, nodded and left the tent.

Jared reached out, gliding strong, darkly tanned hands over the beautiful weave his mother had sewn for their father, the chieftain of this village, who, along with Jared's mother and two sisters, had been ambushed in a village bordering theirs on a raid by the Pharaoh's men. Yes. He wanted their blood on his hands this day.

Revenge.

Yet as he prepared, voices from thousands of years streamed throughout his tent. His mind. His body. All carried a different message and clear warning.

He could hear Sam. The men he'd met in Venice. His own dearly departed parents from England. Mrs. Hoyt. In a rush, he stopped, lifting eyes to heaven. Then he caught the deep voice of a formidable warrior. One who ushered all others from the tent by his mere mystical presence.

"You are not as you seem, Prince Malik. Yet I know all your secrets," was all he could make out as the sound vanished along with the wind.

"Shit. Who was that? All of them? My ancestors?" Prince Malik spoke out loudly as he paced frantically for a few seconds before words from the old crone penetrated his mind, bringing immediate calmness. Then the adrenaline started flowing through as his gut tightened. Apprehension filled Jared's entire being as something yet stronger, more potent, took over.

Excitement. The excitement of the battle.

Placing the tunic over his head, he affixed a woven golden belt around his waist, then strapped on battle sandals. Pulling the knife from the sheath, he ran a finger over the blade, drawing first blood. It was time. His eyes narrowed as he picked up the sword. Everything else would be left behind.

He exited the royal tent for what would be the very last time. He hoped.

The Semite Nation would be proud this day. One way or another. This time he'd follow his instincts instead of ego. It had to turn out differently. Walking over towards the large group of soldiers, he did not pay any heed nor try to comfort with words the sobbing women.

"Men, our choices have been made clear. As we march to battle, keep in your minds why we do this. We will not be held captive, our children segregated, our women scorned and our elders stoned. It is with them in our hearts that we claim back our territory and lives."

Mounted, reins in one hand, he turned and led those on horseback as hundreds of others marched behind, ready to engage their enemy. As the sun moved higher and darkness gave way, they trudged. Up ahead, such a sight came before their front lines.

Charioteers.

Strong, fearless soldiers tightly holding the reins of strong, sleek horses whose hooves pounded the sand beneath them, eager to engage in battle.

It was such a masterful display of strength that

hardly a soul with Prince Malik did not envision being trampled to an unmerciful death. Never had any but one seen such a mechanism as this before.

Fear temporarily immobilized their forces as Prince Malik quickly glanced left and right, knowing swift words had to be spoken.

Ahmall spoke, his voice laden with awe. "Brother, that is the mighty wheeled apparatus Father spoke of when they entered the village. I now know it was what left those deep marks in the dirt we could not identify upon our return."

But Prince Malik knew what had to be done.

"Yes. We will be no match for the likes of this contraption or their swords. Let us not share our thoughts with the others." He glanced around at the men. Those he'd planted fields with, yielded good times, shared a few large jugs of wine and a few women now and again.

"Ahmall, ride to the rear and up to the caves. They must be warned to move on. Do not stop. You must reach them, for there will be carnage and slaughter on this day. Tell them it is my wish they go to the Hebrews. I command it. For word has it they will not be engaged in a battle such as this. They will not lift weapons against Pharaoh's army. Rather, they will be rounded up and expelled. Go with God's speed and be quick."

***

Dust drove high as the single rider could be seen from atop the Egyptian army's encampment. Rano's eyes squinted.

"Awaiting your command."

"Let him go. He will not be able to ride to get reinforcements. There are none. He does not know we made work of them all on the way here. Nor that these are the last remaining villagers alive under Prince Malik's reign. Soon, it will all be as it should."

"It is said he is a great fighter, Prince Malik. But

none can match our great charioteers and your sword and brilliant tactics."

Rano nodded, walking along the ranks at the front lines. But that beautiful little Nofret was on his mind and she had no place there as he prepared for battle. Knowing he had a few minutes, he let his thoughts drift to their last encounter. Her sweet voice had been reliving a tall tale of a great warrior and had held them all spellbound. He soon realized she was talking about him.

For ages, he had tried to get her to pay closer attention to him. Now, he thought, smiling devilishly, it was time. It would not be denied any longer what was between them. They would marry this time. Perhaps she'd give him strong sons and daughters and they all would be taught the fine art of warfare.

So her aloofness had turned to interest and now he was sure it was much more. Good thing. His libido had been sorely tested. Enough was enough. He would have her. No, not by commanding charm as he had done with other women. She was different. With all his tactical training, he knew a better way to get what he so desired from her. Besides, time was running out.

Again.

He kicked a rock, launching it out of the way. "Damn you. Even on the battlefield, you encroach on my thoughts. Be gone. For I proclaim on this day I have no time for you, woman!" His words were harsh as he spewed them into the air. Raising his head high, the fierce mercenary returned, shoving her into the recess. Glancing off at the Semites, he never felt a twinge of guilt at the slaughter that was about to take place. Stepping up onto his chariot, he removed his sword from the sheath, letting it drop to the floorboard, then turned toward his army, honing in on the figure of his rival.

***

Prince Jared's horse stomped its front hooves into

the sand, chomping at the bit to start the pace. Even the horses could feel it. He reined him in and then kicked his sides, raising his spear and shield. The desert sand parted beneath such pressure, leaving a sure imprint on it and the events to follow. It would tell a great story of this fierce battle.

"Attack!" he yelled. His horse and army gathered momentum as the two sides moved closer and closer. As they clashed, he fought on until an enemy soldier's sword clipped his wrist and his sword dropped to the ground below.

Then, as if in a dream, Malik watched one appear as if out of thin air coming straight towards him, smiling to heaven. A large steel handle slid into his palm. It was not one of their own. Quickly, he looked up at this powerful sword, appreciating the fine workmanship before he used it to take down several soldiers, falling to their desert death.

A white-hot sensation suddenly engulfed him as a sword pierced his right side clean through and was pulled out. The reins slipped from his grasp as he lost control of his body. He dropped to the ground even as his mind screamed at him to get up. But it was of no avail. Prince Malik had little strength left now.

The sand absorbed the growing pool of blood, seeming, like Prince Malik, to know it was a losing cause as it streamed around his body. The stinging turned into an ache as his eyes fluttered closed, his body now completely motionless. The pain overtook him and he saw nothing more than a glimmer of her beautiful eyes before blackness flooded his soul.

***

The battle raged on for a few more minutes until the very last Semite left was Ahmall, standing over the lifeless body of his brave, fallen brother. That was where Rano pulled back tightly on the reins of his horse and leaped down, blood dripping from his sword.

Marching straight towards Ahmall, he mercilessly sliced his sword straight through his midsection, pulled it out and wiped it on the tunic of Prince Malik. Not bothering to watch the body fall to the ground, he quickly remounted and circled them both. Brazenly, he reared the horse up on hind legs, released a curdling, victorious battle cry and then riding over the bloodstained earth toward his main army.

"We are a mighty force, men. Work through the village and take what is left. Burn what remains down to the sand before we look in those caves for survivors."

"What are your orders for them?"

"We have done what was asked of us on this day. Gather and keep them alive." He glanced about, nodding as he whirled his horse and entered the village.

"Commander, only a few old men and women remain. I'll take a small band with me up to the caves, by your order."

"Go ahead. Make quick work of it. I do not see much that will be needed here. I will allow those old people to be brought back and settled with the Hebrews. I have seen enough blood today, in truth. I will advise the Pharaoh myself upon return that I made that choice. If he wishes to be angry, he can direct it at me."

Hell, and be damned, he thought. Nofret was back in his mind. How could he slaughter these people and expect her to come to him? She was a healer. It had been very clear to him how appalled she was when they first met and shared a few words. It became important that she realize he was not filled with evil. Perhaps those lovely powers could redeem him. Fill a void no other female had before or since.

Word would spread of this deed. A goodwill gesture towards the old. When she heard, it would be different between them. His horse whinnied as he took the reins in hand. Where had she originally come from? He was fully aware her current village was just downriver on the Nile. Close to one of the palaces. But she was reckless, he knew, traveling often alone from village to village. Healing those in need. Why no husband? Lover? He silently scoffed, thinking *Good thing*. Or he would have had to suddenly make them disappear.

She had visited the palace recently. One of Rano's women had reported back that she had not seen the queen. Instead, she had visited a local sage. He wanted to get back and delve into this, into her, more as the thrill of the day receded.

Pulling back on the reins, he dismounted. Taking a torch, he ignited the prince's tent. *Bastard*. Finally, he was out of his life and his sight, he thought as a sly grin came across his devilishly good-looking face.

"Have fifty of the men gather the livestock and prepare the caravan for departure. Abbore, take twenty to the caves and confirm they are indeed vacated. Then, we move out."

In less than an hour the village was burned. Those foolish enough to run for it or remain hidden in caves were surrounded, surrendered and brought around to see reason. Everything was looted and claimed, including the animals, as they marched back toward the barges that would take them all to the other royal palace at Memphis, upriver on the Nile.

***

As the ravens started to peck away at the dead bodies, a small group that had avoided detection by Rano's army started their descent from the caves. In utter disbelief they met, staring down at the horrifying sight below. Rushing, they began the awful task of checking each fallen soldier from their village.

"Over here. This one is alive. Barely. I just heard him groan. Help me get him up and onto the cart. Maybe the healer can help. Hurry."

"We've checked," another replied. "There are no other survivors. I have given instructions for several to remain behind and start the burial process. What shall we do after that? Follow the army back toward the Nile?"

"No, we shall go and blend in with the Hebrews and perhaps another time we will rise up again. We are not finished as a race. Not yet."

Chapter Two

"I need you to use your knife and cut away the cloth. I must see how much blood he has lost and if I can save him. Someone was watching over this poor soul. That is for sure. If he was not so well draped with this linen, he would have bled more and died on the battlefield. The weave staunched the flow."

"Healer, I am afraid to pull on this piece. It is blended with the blood and wound. It has dried on. If I do, it may start again."

"Put your finger on the edge, here. I will pull as hard as I can. Better be prepared for a struggle if he has an ounce of life left in his dirty, battered body. You ready?" The woman nodded, placing a knee over his legs. "Yes, do it now while I still have the nerve."

Nofret lifted the edge with a fingernail. When she had enough in it, she tugged with lightning-quick force. The man launched straight up, knocking her backward onto a hip. Then he fell, moaning in pain.

Nofret took in his appearance. His beard was thick and heavy, encased with dirt. Quickly washing out the wound, she had no choice but to scrub it with sea salt. That would sting like hell, but it needed to be done. Prepared, she took a deep breath and began.

"Quick, put a glob of the aloe and olive treatment onto the wound. That's good. Now help me lift him so I can look at his back."

The two women struggled but managed to get him upright. "It is as I thought. It did penetrate through his shoulder and out the back. Hand me the bandages. Now hold him tight while I wrap these around. We need to get him as comfortable as possible before he wakes up. That is, if he wakes up."

Gingerly, it took them both to settle him back onto the makeshift blankets. "There is no doubt that a fever will be forthcoming. How long, I'm not sure. But we must be diligent and keep a watchful eye on him. Bring me the jars. I'll mix up what I need and see if I can get some of it into him in a drink. I want you to come back in two hours and relieve me, Dahlia. I feel sad he's the only one that survived out of them all. Surely it was for a reason unknown to us. If he does pass, at least we can ensure he's as comfortable as possible."

"Healer, I will. If anyone can work magic and save him, it is you. I'll go now and take care of things. Then I'll be back. The guard is outside the flap if you need him. Rapidly news is passing around the village. Someone is here who witnessed the battle from a secluded cave. It is true that this was at the hands of Rano the Mercenary. The king was not there during the assault."

Nofret glanced up, nodding as her eyes glazed over. "Stories of his great battlefield skills and tactics do not hold any favor with me, Dahlia. But yes, I am fully aware he shows an interest in me. Now go. Stop all this jabber. We will not be discussing him further while we care for this poor, sick old man."

Moving over to the jars, she mixed a powder for him to drink, adding it slowly to the wine and watching as it dissolved. *That should assist in it going down easily combined with a concoction of dill, apple, and balsam. Plus a bit of honey and mint to ease any discomfort that may arise in his stomach.* This mixture would work well to aid in the release of any fever. But she had no doubt one was to follow.

It was going to be a tough stretch for him over the next several days. She'd do the best she could, she thought, nodding over at the statue of *Sekhmet*, the healing goddess of Upper Egypt. "Please help if you can. You know how I feel about all of this. If you can hear me, know I am sincere for his sake. Surely, he must have been saved so this story could be told for generations to come. I give you my plight."

She lifted his head and got him to drink the wine without spitting it back in her face. Every few minutes she repeated the process until the goblet was emptied. "There, that will help you, Semite." She mixed up another one and set it aside. Later, this routine would continue until she was relieved.

Stepping out into the open, Nofret nodded at the guard, who she now knew had been there for two days. A special appointment by the great wife of Thutmose III, Satiah, who by special courier had requested her presence as soon as duties in the village allowed. The guard would then be Nofret's guide and protector to the palace. Unclear as to why, the note had not revealed what the queen wanted. It only read: "Nofret Qalhata, Healer, come to me. I have a need of your workings. Be here as soon as possible."

Two men had arrived. One stayed and one was sent back with her hand-written reply advising of the sick that needed attending. She would rush there as soon as it was clear whether one requiring constant attention survived or not. Until then, she remained the queen's faithful servant.

She burned the original note. It was partly in disgust at such a random command, when the queen housed her own sages and mysterious healers at the palace. Nofret was fully aware, from having been in that vicinity, that the queen had an entire entourage that followed her every step. But also for privacy. No one else needed to know her own private business or that of the queen's.

Continuing by the guard and inhaling a deep breath of fresh air, her mind drifted to a sage that had lived temporarily up in one of the caves who had also sent a cryptic message warning Nofret to pay attention to everything happening around her now. To not be stubborn about the advances of one man and to keep distance with another. Properly forewarned and forearmed, Nofret felt as if she was walking on hot coals. Who was the second man? She truly was not aware of another that sought her out so blatantly as Rano during the months she had been here.

A soft moan from inside brought her back in a rush. Taking a linen cloth and saturating it in fresh well-water drawn just that morning, she sponged his clammy brow.

Already the mixture was working to expel the fever from his battered body. She glanced back at the partially open flap and saw the sun had set. Dahlia would be returning shortly, so she held his head up again in her hand while managing to get a second goblet finished.

Mixing another, she set it down as Dahlia entered. "Right on time. I have given him two doses. That will ease through his body and calm his mind for a few more hours. When the sweats and shaking begin, give him the mixture in that goblet. Then pat his head, neck, and chest down with cloth and water. I'm pretty confident that this will see him through the night." She scooted a scorpion under an opening and back outside.

"Damn things, never liked them. Anyway, stay with him. We need to find out who he is and what we are to do with him. His recuperation will take quite a while. I think possibly six or seven days. Don't relay under any circumstances what he tells you or mumbles in a heightened fever. I trust you, Dahlia. Don't let anyone persuade you that our business with him is also theirs."

Nofret brushed a hand against his beard as a slight tingle weaved up her spine. She stood, glancing down at him with her eyes narrowing.

"Healer, you have my word."

"Good. I am on my out of the village. I have been requested elsewhere. Four times over the next several days remix the drink and herbs. Change his dressing and reapply new salve twice a day. I will let one of the younger girls know they are to bring you food and drink. You can step outside. But stay close in case he wakes. We don't want him being injured further. Also, make sure the crawlers keep out of the tent. They seem to always locate the sickest of the sort and sting them with their poison."

Dahlia nodded. "When will you return back to us?"

"I don't know. Once I am there and hear what is needed of me, I will have a better understanding. I know you figured it out. Some of the others here have as well. I can tell by their glances at the guard. His uniform clearly gives it away. But let's not discuss that. We know he is the queen's. The less speculation involved will benefit us all."

A sly grin appeared on Nofret's face. "Has he even blinked?"

The two women smiled.

"Yes, he let one of the women bring him food and drink. He's staunch, I give him that. He has only left his post toward the bushes a few times. He's a man of steel."

They giggled.

"Okay." She picked up her carpet satchel. "I'm off. I entrust him to you. If for some reason things turn out bad, make sure they bury him and not burn him."

Dahlia nodded. "Safe travels there and back, Nofret."

"Thank you. Good luck with him. Pray to Sekhmet while I am away." Her grin grew as she nodded, hand holding the tent flap open. "Oh, and Dahlia, if anyone does come snooping about, we do not know his identity. We are waiting for his fever to break so we can discern who he is. I made sure to dispose of certain things already." With that, she walked out of the tent, the flap dropping behind her, and stared straight into the eyes of her new companion.

His stoic face, leathery, tanned and lined with tell-tale creases around his eyes, told her he was indeed a weathered soldier. Hardly acknowledging Nofret at all, he was standing by, prepared to help her mount if needed. As if on command, the camel knelt and she climbed on, grabbing the ropes. As the bag was secured, she patted his long neck and the animal slowly rose.

Nofret smiled. The slow and gentle pitch and rocking sensation swayed her around. But she enjoyed it. Camels were a necessity in the deserts of Egypt and the Middle East. She had always loved these gentle giants of the desert and was very much at home on them. From here they would trek a few miles, then board a beautifully crafted wooden boat bearing the queen's crest as they sailed up the Nile. She knew their arrival would be at the second largest of their royal palaces in Memphis.

Of course he did not speak. He rode beside her, never taking his eyes off the areas they passed through, vigilantly ensuring no one would halt their progress. She doubted any group of bandits would even try. Indeed, he was hardly a regular foot soldier. As she glanced more than once over at him, she knew he would be nearly as formidable as Rano.

Quite handsome, his tunic was of red and gold. Sandals, partially covered with royal armor, ascended up his legs, stopping just below his knees. Yes, he was indeed privileged. But she was sure he had earned it through blood, sweat, and determination. She pondered how the women would gather around him when he arrived back to where he was stationed. This type of man never had lonely nights. Of that, Nofret was sure.

He did, though, glance her way just once as a slight flush crept into her cheeks. Steadying her gaze ahead, Nofret watched the brilliant blue of the Nile become clearer as they reached the thriving village where the boat was awaiting their departure. As the camel kneeled and she slid off, the soldier took her bag and motioned with one hand for her to proceed him up the gang-plank.

At the stern on the top deck, she sat, noticing the

bag had been set down close by. He remained near, leaning against a railing as his eyes searched the snaking river.

"How long will the journey on this vessel be?"

He turned, coming over. "Through two sunsets, then we will arrive. The winds feel strong against our back. Look at how the reeds bend over on the other shore. If it remains that way, we will have a quick sail."

She smiled up into those handsome features as one of his brows raised in silent amusement. She kept it to herself that she was amazed he had disclosed so much. The entire camel ride he had not uttered one damn single word. Indeed, men here could be harder to read than in the future. When had things changed?

Over his shoulder she surveyed a woman heading toward them, carrying a very heavy wooden tray. As she neared, Nofret's stomach grumbled. Laid before her were meats, fruit, two wine goblets and bread. She motioned her closer. "You can set that down next to me."

"No, she won't. Woman, don't listen to her. Set it by my side. Then go. We will not be in need your services until I advise."

The servant quickly scurried off.

Interesting, Nofret thought. She was a pretty woman. But he had treated her like she was beneath his feet. "Why did you do that? If I may be so bold to ask."

He lifted the wine, pouring a small amount and tasting it. Filling the other goblet, he handed it to her. "To ensure you are not poisoned."

"Oh. Did the queen request that of you?"

"No, Rano did."

Drinking down more than she should have, Nofret spewed out a small amount that landed at his sandals.

"Something wrong?" His mirth was clear.

Damn ass, she wanted to say. "No. Just a bit bitter, that's all."

She watched as he tasted everything off the platter

and then set it down on the cyprus wood stool at her feet. "You can eat."

"Won't you have any?"

"I just did."

Once again, he was baiting her. "Are you looking for some kind of an argument so you can report back to your commander what a nasty woman I am?"

"He would not believe it so. I'm testing you for my own knowledge. He only speaks highly of you. Only here I doubt him. Surely, no woman could manipulate the greatness of Rano the Mercenary."

"Oh, you are so full of shit."

He laughed so loud it brought several glances from those working on the ship. "Now that's better. He said you have a quick tongue and sharp mind."

"I think you got that backward. Just wait until some woman gets into your head and you lose all rational thought. I'm going to make sure I see this happen."

"Healer, the sun will stop shining over Egypt when that occurs."

They both laughed.

"Don't be so sure. Someplace out there she exists. It's only a matter of time before you two meet."

He leaned down, resting an arm on a strong upper thigh. She truly had to lock eyes with his to not look at what might lurk beneath his clothing.

"I've been through almost all the household women in the palace and I can assure you she's not there."

Nofret popped a grape into her mouth. "Nope, you are right. She is not. But she does exist. I can see her. You will fall to your knees begging for her attention one day. Mark my words." It was bullshit, but she wanted to tease this soldier a bit longer.

His grin was devilish, and now inches from her face. "Woman, you lie. Now I am beginning to realize Rano's torment."

She smiled up seductively, eyes ablaze. "I was just delaying your exit from my company to make sure the food and drink are safe. That's all."

He slapped the railing, grinning all the way to the ladder below deck. There, he would indeed eat and drink. Just not in her presence.

She ate, enjoying the journey on this fine vessel. The simple, smooth rhythm of the oars being pulled up, over and down into the water in a repeating pattern, was soothing her mind. She watched with eager interest as a group of men raised the sails. The wind took them and they billowed out.

Bread raised to take a bite, she halted, recalling a larger, sleeker ship that she had seen in a recent dream. A skull and bones flag flew high above a lookout point. Then it was gone.

How she loved life on the Nile. It was her home. Her lifestyle was gentle, being a healer. But she did have to leave at times the comfort of her village in Middle Egypt and go where no healer lived. She had to wonder why Queen Satiah wanted her when there was a full host of sages, alchemists, and herbalists at her disposal in the royal household.

She set the goblet down, never partaking in that much drink, as she nodded for the hovering woman to come and take it away. She rose, stretching her legs as the vessel cut swiftly through the darkening waters of the Nile.

He was back up on deck, having finished his meal, Nofret assumed, as without hesitation she approached him. "I don't suppose it is allowed to ask if you have any idea why our queen wants to see me?"

"No, I do not know. I just follow orders."

"Well, it was worth an ask." He seemed preoccupied now as his gaze glanced back towards the vacated chair and then towards her. "Oh, you don't want to talk now. Is that it?"

He started to open his mouth to speak, but she was quick to interrupt whatever he was going to say. "All right. I shall go sit. On second thought, I won't. It looks like one of the servant women is trying to get my attention."

The woman nodded her toward a partially tented-off area in the middle of the boat. "We have made a make-shift bed for you. It should be comfortable. I will stay here with you. If you need anything just ask. Tomorrow we will arrive at the palace and the queen would wish to see you refreshed."

"Oh, that's sooner than I was told. Okay, good. Thank you. If you do not mind my asking, what is your name?"

"Ospera, and yes, you are correct that we will arrive ahead of schedule. This journey is blessed by strong winds."

"That's pretty. Your name I mean. Do you happen to know why the queen has asked for me? I inquired with my escort, but he is not aware."

"I do. But it is for her to tell you. Not me." She swept a single hand around the small enclosed area. "Will this work for your needs?" She had moved the draped linen panel down so they were indeed enclosed. Nofret settled on the cushions and was covered with a blanket.

"Yes, with this pitching of the ship and listening to the oars and the wind, I think I will actually sleep. Thank you, Ospera."

"Good dreams to you, Healer Nofret."

"Thank you." Within minutes she dozed off, falling into a very deep sleep.

Suddenly, men's voices alerted her that she must have slept longer than she realized. Glancing over, she saw that Ospera had left a damp cotton cloth. Nofret reached for it and washed hands and face. She would leave her hair unbound, never having been one of those that wore the popular black wigs of this period.

But she did reach inside her bag and apply her very own mixture of alluring scents and oils where the wind would catch it just right and take it upon the breeze. Perhaps all the way to Rano. Shaking her head at such frivolous thoughts, she tied up the bag and sat quietly for a few moments in contemplative meditation.

But it was short lived.

Ospera poked her head inside. "It is nearly mid-day, healer. You slept longer than I thought."

She grinned. "Yes. You should have woken me. I feel like I wasted part of my day."

Ospera shrugged. "You needed the rest and may not have as much once we reach the palace. So I left you alone. Besides, there is not much one can do on this ship but watch the water, birds flocking above or the men."

"Ah, there are indeed some interesting options, then."

They laughed softly.

"There are food and drink where your chair is and the sun is bright and warm against today's breeze. We still have a strong one and expect to be arriving as planned when the sun sets."

Ospera held back the makeshift drape as Nofret stood, walking out into the bright sunshine. It took a couple of seconds for her eyes to adjust. "You are right. Indeed, it is a lovely day. I'm not familiar with this area of the Nile. Where do we pass?"

"The shores of Herakleopolis."

She sat down, taking food off the platter to her left while sipping on the wine. That was why she'd slept so well last night. It was probably due to the two cups she had consumed. Although not drunk, it was as if she had taken a sleeping draft and it had mellowed her mood.

She turned to say something, but Ospera had returned to the draping. With the assistance of one of the men, she took it down and folded it. She then disappeared once again below the deck.

As the current, wind and men manning the oars moved them farther up the river, three hours later off in the distance, she began to see the brilliant torches signaling the end of this journey.

It was as if she was in a dream observing the cool shades of marble and granite steps as they rose from the waters of the Nile. Appearing to be suspended from the very heavens, pools of flowering lotus blossoms danced across the ripples of the water stirred slightly by a light breeze. Their heavy scent wafted up just as her first sandal stepped onto the marble.

Two women were awaiting her arrival. She took in the sheer gauze wraps that tried to house their bodies, but in the disappearing sunshine, they were clearly outlined for all to see. Did they expect her to dress like that? She grinned, knowing that would have quite an effect on Rano the Great.

They rushed down to take her bag, clutching both her arms as they ushered her up the stairs and onto the landing. As they walked beneath four grand pillars, Nofret glanced about, marveling in true awe at what was before her. Halting them both by her quick stop, she was allowed a moment to gaze at all the glory and splendor around her before their giggles motivated her to move along with them.

Rapidly, their infectious laughter gave way to seductive smiles as a small band of soldiers exited the king's wing just as they passed.

"Good to see you, Healer Qalhata."

She nodded at Rano, eyeing him skeptically at this impeccable timing. Then she kept right on walking. *Damn*, she thought, *I should have acted more politely.* But the truth was women were not allowed in public to openly display any emotions in front of the men. *Especially that man*, she thought. One thing was clear. She'd not be able to avoid him now.

In truth, she did not want to.

"We have your rooms ready, healer. There will be a massage later. But see here, there is plenty of food, drink, and music to keep you occupied. It is imperative that you have a good night's rest before your appointment with the queen scheduled for later in the morning tomorrow. She rises early to take an oil bath in the private pools. After that, she will want to see you."

Former kings and queens beautifully carved out of stone lined the final three steps up into her rooms. The double-wide wooden doors suddenly swung open as women of various ages rushed out towards her. Hands. All Nofret could feel were hands all over her. Pulling, tugging, removing her clothing, pushing her down onto a set of oversized plush silk pillows.

Those hands continued, removing the silk band from her long hair. Another took both of her sandals. Then off in the distance, growing louder, was beautiful music being played by a lone woman with a golden harp. Each stroke of the strings brought Nofret to a quieter, more gentle place inside her head. The sound was positively lovely.

Yes. She could get used to this. Being in the desert all the time with constant dirt in the teeth did not always sit well. Or taste well. Then again, out there she was with her people. Those that could not ever dream of this and who needed her special healing magic to help them just to survive.

But it was a lot more than that.

Out there was freedom.

Rising naked, unabashed, her beautiful body was exposed to strangers, a hand clasping one of hers as she followed in a languid trance.

"Healer Qalhata, come into the pool. We will wash your hair, set it and then massage your body with essential oils. You will have the very best of the queen's delights tonight."

Running the clear water through her hands, she let them do just as they would. When those subtle fingers began easing tired muscles, Nofret fell into a deep, sound sleep.

Giggling woke her. *Damn these pesky people*, she thought. Could they not leave her alone for two straight minutes?

"Healer Qalhata, we are sorry. You must get up so we can dress you."

She eyed what one of them was holding. Was that slim, soft, pink gauze material going to cover her enough? She'd need more clothes than that to see the queen, that was clear. "Will I have something different to wear tomorrow?"

They appeared to be amused by her question. Did they think her just a simple healer, not caring about what she wore because she lived predominantly in the desert?

Oh, she thought, finding amusement now with their lack of her background completely. *If they only knew*. They were basing this on that ugly tunic she'd used to arrive in. A sly grin passed by her lips. She let them dress her in it and then slid under the soft, smooth sheets. A sigh escaped of its own accord.

Two very young maidens stood outside the silky mesh drapes surrounding the oversized bed. As her lids drooped, she shook awake, remembering they were still there. "You can go. I will not need you to stay here all night." At their hesitation, she persisted. "It is my wish. Queen Satiah will be fine with my decision and should she question me, I will let her know I felt so safe I did not believe you were needed to watch over me. Good night, ladies."

A bit later when she rolled to a side, one eye barely opened. But it was enough to know they were gone. Early the next morning, just as a phoenix flew over the wing of rooms, Nofret woke. Stretching languishingly like a sleek, satisfied black cat, she opened her eyes to scan the area. Six women stood around her bed, ready to pounce and prepare her for the queen.

"Okay. So here you are." She did not know what else to say. Had they arrived with orders not to wake her? This moment was a bit embarrassing, even for her. "I'm all yours."

With all tasks completed, Nofret's eyes roamed over the flowing aqua silk tunic tied snugly with a glistening gold belt. A small shudder passed through her, though, as she noticed the mesmerizing blue lapis lazuli stones encased on her leather sandals.

It was his stone. A stone of royalty. Visions of long ago, yet they were now, beamed through her third eye like she was watching it happen live. In a split second, she saw a quick flash of a strange wooden object suspended off the ground with legs then vanished. "What the…" she started, and then stopped as a soft gasp from one of the women reached her ears.

A potent internal struggle then began in earnest. Shrugging, she smiled, acknowledging the hard work they had just put into making her more than presentable for the queen. They had made her beautiful. Later when there was more time and privacy, Nofret would do a card reading and see if what she had just experienced could be made clear. For now, she had to let it go.

As she followed one of the ladies out of her room, the breeze from the open corridors weaved through her garment, gently caressing her skin. A soft quiver of delicious delight ran up her spine. The scent of lotus, rose and jasmine assaulted her senses, the queen's own special scent. Its arrival announced her long before she made her grand entrance.

"Ladies, we will need some time alone. Go and bring us back our meal and then leave us. I will let you know when to return. Healer Qalhata, come. Sit opposite me on the pillows so we can have our much-needed talk."

Nofret lowered herself and got comfortable. "Is it permissible to ask you a question?"

"Of course. Here we speak without barriers."

"I must admit at wondering why I've been invited to see you with all the excellent people you have here, my Queen."

"You shall have your answer. Word has spread to me of your amazing uses of the herbs. There are those here and in the caves high up in the hills that cannot replicate some of your idolized potions." She leaned closer, taking both of Nofret's hands in a tight grip. "My king and I are having a bit of trouble producing our first heir. I had my sage provide my forecast and she talked of Nofret from the middle village of Amama, who has special gifts blessed upon her by the Goddess Hathor."

Nofret had heard these rumblings even within her own village and others during the last moon cycle. "You do indeed honor me with such talk. I am your servant, always. What would you ask of me?"

"The king is preparing to march with the charioteers and army to western Asia. When their business is concluded, they will continue to Ethiopia in three moons. It is my hope that when he leaves, I will have blessed him with the news of an upcoming child. A son. Tell me you can make this possible."

This powerful woman, strong of spirit and heart, fair and honorable, was asking her above all others for help.

"Yes, I can. I have seen this in a vision before leaving my village. I am prepared to assist. We can begin right away. I brought my herbs and oils in the carpet bag." The healer leaned closer to her to ask, "When was your last bleeding?"

"Five days."

"Excellent. I will need some glass bowls and sticks.

Where do you want me to work? I will require a room with a plentiful breeze so I can capture the wind off the Nile. Also, along with that, I ask for lotus and jasmine buds. Unfortunately, I used my supply and did not have enough time to gather more to bring."

The women returned with food and drink and set it before them. "Meliah, stay and get a papyrus, reed, and ink. Write some items down for me. Then go to the market and secure them. When you have gathered the highest quality, bring them to the small chambers behind my quarters and come and let us know. We will be here or at the pools."

When she returned with the writing materials, Nofret dictated a list of exactly what was required. Promptly, the servant left the palace toward the village market.

"How long will it take before we have news?"

"Well, I can tell you that before he leaves we will have an answer." She would not insult this woman by asking if she had been praying to the goddess herself. Of course, the sage would have suggested that a long time ago when they had been unsuccessful. Although they had only been wed two years, it was a bit unusual that she had not successfully conceived by now. Then again, Nofret had seen visions of a future filled with difficulties for them.

"Shall we swim?" the queen asked. "The waters today are warmer in the pool as there was no chill last night." They talked easily along the way.

"I would like that. I noticed how beautiful it is here. When I was in the village near the palace at Thebes, I did not have a chance to see all the temples. There are quite a few here. There their numbers are greater. Is that correct?"

"Yes, more than any other city in the New Kingdom. When you wish to come back, send a note ahead and I will welcome you into our palace so you will not have to stay in the village. Although it has been advised to me that you much prefer the dust of the desert and a simpler way of life."

"Indeed, I do. But at times like this, I am also happy to be out of them." They both laughed. "Yes, one could truly get used to this, my Queen."

They were assisted in disrobing and quietly slipped into the pools overlooking the Nile. Adorned with her luscious glittering eye makeup and dark wig glistening in the sun, Queen Satiah was indeed a beauty that would stop any man in his tracks.

Over her head, Nofret caught sight of the one she now knew as Meliah approaching at a near run. She tried not to break out laughing. Bowing to them both, Meliah looked at Nofret. "We have gathered everything on your list and are ready. Would you like to begin now?"

"Yes. If my queen will allow me to leave her company?"

Her response was a simple nod followed by a gentle smile.

Nofret snapped her fingers and her wrap reappeared as she climbed out of the pool, was dried off with rough linen and flax and dressed. Bowing, she left the queen, who was now resting her head back on a pillow, eyes searching the heavens above. Or perhaps beseeching. Nofret was not sure.

Chapter Three

She was brought into a pair of large rooms that were wide, open and airy. Outside, abutting both, were several beautifully white-washed patios. Further, she had her own pools and garden, overflowing with various herbs and flowers. It was lovely and Nofret sighed, wishing she had such extravagances back in the village. There were times when this would indeed be useful in healing those that required it. Supplies here were more abundant.

Walking back inside, she saw that two women stood, intently watching her every move. The sheerest of drapes hung to keep some of the flying insects out as her eyes drew to the cushions where she would spend the next several nights. Turning back, she smiled at them. "This will do very well. I know I am not too far from the queen's rooms. Which will prove vitally important when I have the potions ready to deliver. Go ahead and unpack. I'll let you know where I want my supplies. It will be in the other room. I can work in there away from my night chamber."

Her few articles of clothing were neatly folded and set into a bamboo basket. How ironic that she carried more herbs and oils than clothing. The other woman picked up her carpet bag, setting things in their proper place, and nodded for Nofret to follow.

"I think you will find everything within close reach. We are now ready. What other requisites do you have?"

"A large jug of water from the Nile. But do not have it drawn until just as the sun sets. It is imperative that the timing is exact. Not one minute before or after the sun disappears into the water. It must shine as if diamonds glisten upon it." Nofret glanced up at the sky. "There is still some time prior to that occurring. You will need a reliable man for this. The quantity expected necessitates a big, strong man for this task. But you must be right there with him, making sure it is not removed one minute early or late. Then bring it back to me. I leave you with these instructions to take care of when the time is right. In the meanwhile, I would like some soft music played outside these rooms. But no singing, please. All I desire is quiet distraction."

Nofret pointed toward the other women. "Please do not move the palm fronds any longer. The breeze coming in is sufficient. Shortly I will be grinding powders. I do not want to take a chance any of it is displaced by such a motion. If you want you can sit. When I need your assistance, I will ask."

She lined up all the soft and hard ingredients and began moving about the chamber mixing, grinding and adding them into a larger mortar. When the correct level had been reached, she placed them into a black cauldron suspended over a wood-burning pit. "I also ask for blocks of myrrh and cedar resin along with three bundles of papyrus. Go ahead now and retrieve them."

The woman in the chair rose and Nofret caught a brief glimpse of dissatisfaction upon the younger girl's features.

"I apologize. That was rude of me. Please tell me your name?"

"Asofia, healer."

"Pretty name. Thank you for helping me."

"It's for our queen. For her, I would move heaven and earth." She started from the rooms but Nofret halted her. "The other woman is Meliah, I believe. Am I correct? I heard her name spoken by the queen and previously when I saw her in the market. But want to make sure."

"You are right."

Nofret looked closely at her now. She seemed anxious to move on.

"Anything else? If not, I will go."

"Nothing. Thank you."

When all was in order, Nofret moved out to glance at the Nile. The sun was starting to set and Meliah was down on the steps with the soldier, a jug between them, ready to be filled. *Good*, Nofret thought, satisfied at their progress while moving back in. Asofia returned shortly with all the other items. "I will have food and drink brought when you are ready."

"Thank you." At the pit she stacked the wood and resin, having them touch at the top and fan out at the bottom. Smiling, she recalled back in Norway how she had learned this from that rogue, Gunner. It was the surest way to keep a fire going. Shaking her head and shoving those thoughts back into the recesses of her mind, she manipulated the papyrus into a cone shape, keeping it adhered by a bit of spit.

Moving the cauldron's arm, she knelt, eyeing the distance from the flame. *Yes*, she thought, it would work. Removing mixtures from all three glass jars and emptying them into the bottom, she turned, raising eyes to the heavens and silently offering up gratitude at the success of this ceremonial process. The timing was perfect.

The guard, followed close at hand by Meliah, parted the draping and entered with the jug filled with the water from the ancient Nile.

"You can set it down right next to me. You are free to go. I will need you to meet Meliah over the next two nights. The exact same time and procedure. If you are unable, let me know now. I must have someone completely reliable to assist her."

"I am at your service, healer, by orders of the queen."

"Excellent. Thank you."

He bowed, thumping his right fist on his chest, and left the chambers.

She ignited the wood and resin with sage brush and set it into the center of the circle on top of the blocks. It exploded to life, crackling sparks flying upwards. Stepping back, simultaneously mesmerized, mouths agape with eyes wide, both women watched in complete concentration, totally drawn in by the healer's display of magic. It confirmed all the stories they had both heard.

Reaching for the large, blue jar, Nofret immersed it into the jug filled with the Nile water and spilled it into the cauldron. Hissing smoke billowed straight up, then dispersed on the breeze and filled the room. Repeating the whole process two more times, she then mixed it slowly. Using the long glass rod, she stopped intermittently as if in a trance. Then inhaled the thick concoction while softly chanting words neither girl would understand.

"It is ready. Bring me that glass vial and remove the stopper. Hurry now. Time is of the essence."

She dipped the blue jar into the cauldron and quickly filled the vial, sealing it immediately. Walking over to the edge of the patio, she held the vial up to the moon, her body swaying back and forth. Turning, she nodded to the women.

"Take me to her now."

They walked silently at a quickened pace, together.

At the queen's doors, Nofret met with no delay and was immediately allowed entry.

Getting ready to meet the king for their evening feast, the queen stopped. She never took her eyes off the healer as Nofret approached.

"Accept this now. Before your meal. You will find it is bitter but palpable."

"Taste it before me. I have to be sure about you."

Quickly uncorking it, Nofret took a tiny amount onto her tongue and swallowed it. "You are safe with me, my Queen."

The queen's fingers clasped it firmly, tipped the

contents back and drank until the glass vial was empty. "Do you want this back?"

"Yes." Nofret took it. "Tonight you will make love with your husband. We will repeat this entire sequence in the exact order over the following two nights. Then you will go and visit the sage to be delivered your awaited news."

Nofret took a step backward to leave. "I will then depart for my village. You will send me word of confirmation. The Pharaoh will know before he travels that you are expecting your first son. All the land will share in your joy. He will be healthy. He will sit on his father's throne when the day comes."

The queen nodded. A lovely, knowing smile hovered upon her face. "As you say it, so it shall be. It is now declared by you, Healer Nofret. You may now go."

The ladies escorted her back to the chambers. "I wish to have a platter and drink brought to me shortly. I will not need you both until tomorrow. Later in the afternoon. As I mentioned to the queen, I say to you both as well. Same time, the same process. See you tomorrow. Thank you."

When the food arrived, she ate and walked out from the rooms laughing to herself. For the queen indeed trusted her. But not completely. Just outside was an assigned guard to keep watch on her comings and goings. *Fine*, she thought, reconciled to the reasons why. But she'd not stay put. If he was to guard her, then he was going to go on a nighttime stroll. Like it or not.

Coming across a beautiful marble pond, she watched, enchanted by lotus dancing animatedly against the vibrantly lit stars in the sky above. Sitting down and crossing her legs, she glanced off into the distance. He was there. A gray silhouette against the darkening night. Closing her eyes, she fell deeply in prayer. Holding palms up, facing the fuller moon, she spoke with the cat-faced goddess of fertility and motherhood, Bast.

Even deep in meditation, Nofret saw visions of her guard appointed by the queen watching her every move. She was fully aware his eyes were gazing upon her lightly clad attire. The moon shone down upon her, revealing to his eyes all her curves.

She suppressed a grin, took a deeper breath and settled more deeply into prayer. After nearly thirty minutes, she finally lowered her hands and opened her eyes to see he had now moved from the shadows and was standing a few feet in front of her leaning against a closer pillar.

Nofret rose and they walked side by side. "I think you would be better rid of me now for want of food, drink, and other pleasures?" She smiled up into his handsome face and ruggedly chiseled features, seeing desire in those eyes. "I know you are ordered by the queen to watch over me. But you could visit the ladies down the hall in my wing. I'm sure they would enjoy company this night. I doubt they are allowed to take of such pleasures with their current responsibilities. This could prove to be a satisfying situation. If you know what I mean?"

They arrived back at her rooms, where she lowered the flimsy drapes, providing some privacy. More than that, it also seemed to keep the night creatures from paying an unwanted visit. Damn, how she detested those pesky scorpions. She watched on in amusement at what he was doing.

He surveyed the interior rooms, checking for ghosts lurking in the shadows, she imagined. Finally satisfied, he spoke at last.

"It was my orders to stay with you until daylight when they join you. I cannot disobey those."

"Ah, I see. I shall not compromise you then, but have an idea." She came out, then marched down the long, quiet hallway. Halting at their shared chamber, she opened one door, rather boldly, to the two ladies' startled expressions.

"I have need of volunteers to come and pass the evening away with my guard. I can't have him bored all night outside my rooms. I have two separate chambers opposite each other. If this warrants your interest, ladies, please come and help him out."

She turned, leaving them as four jumped to their bare feet and were quickly on her heels.

Walking over and parting the sheer gauzy drapes, she motioned him inside. "Over in there. You will not have abandoned me. In fact, being inside puts you closer to protecting me than out there. Enjoy your night, soldier."

Could a man's grin be bigger than that? Nofret thought.

He nodded, glancing back only once at the wisdom of her words as with purposeful strides she watched him move out of sight and directly into the other chamber. Rich, deep laughter followed by soft sighs and giggles was all she could hear while climbing back into the plush bed.

Gentle hands slid over supple silk sheets as she released a truly contented sigh. For once, it felt good to send a bit of pleasure their way. For once it felt good to not have to heal someone who was sick. For once it felt good to not see glimpses in her mind's eye of another who still haunted bits and pieces of her life here.

Listening to the babble of a fountain off in the distance, Nofret allowed her tired mind to claim her tired body and sleep.

The next morning, she rose to sounds coming from their direction. Catching sight of him before he disappeared, she gave him a knowing smile. Without a doubt, he would have a good day and quite possibly look forward to leaving his regular military duties to come back again the next two nights.

As she was bathed in the pool and redressed, she noticed something behind one of the lady's backs and nodded her over, extending a hand.

"You have a note from the village, Healer Nofret." The rolled papyrus was grabbed, opened and the script read. "In a feverish state, he has spoken. It is not broken yet. But it should this night or by the morning. I have news for you. When shall you return?"

She nodded at one of the girls. "Bring me a reed brush and ink. I will write a reply and have it taken back to my village. The delivery needs to be quick. It must be handed to the same person that sent it to me. I need your promise."

When she returned, Nofret wrote the reply: "Two more nights and my needs here will have been met. I shall see you the day after tomorrow. Give him an extra dose this evening and tomorrow if needed. I assure you that will flush the fever from his body."

She let it dry in the sun, rolled it back up and handed it to Meliah. "Please see it is brought there now. By the way, how was this delivered? Surely not by the same river route I took to come here?"

"No, healer. By courier on horseback. He rode straight through to you. He has been replaced by a fresh rider and horse awaiting your return note, should there be one. I will make sure he is on his way in minutes."

"Thank you." She took it as Nofret glanced at Asofia.

"You have a question for me burning on your tongue. Do not be afraid to speak. What is it?"

Asofia came closer, glancing around, ensuring no one would be lurking in the shadows. "You are very young and quite beautiful. How did you learn all the trades of one that should be an elder?"

That brought out a laugh. Sometimes stories had to be embellished. "By birth. I was born with special talents that I noticed when I started to walk. My instincts are in line with the gods and goddesses. I can hear those from the heavens. They help me heal wherever I am at the time. They guide me. But we are all special, Asofia. Give this some thought. If you were not here right now, doing as I request, exactly in the proper order, things would not have the same outcome. Would they? You are equally as important. Our queen needs you just as she needs me. Not one sitting above the other."

"Oh. I had not thought of that." She lowered her head, blushing. That flush creeping up her cheeks certainly had not been caused by Nofret's reply. That was apparent. It was the remnants of what had occurred during the passing night.

"You had your fill of him last night. I can see it written all over you today. Well, you had better rest until I need you again. For I have it on excellent authority he will return tonight. Plus, one more following. I am sure he will be searching you out again."

"Oh, healer, if I may be so bold. Indeed, he is a handsome man. Full of energy, strength, and stamina. We all enjoyed him."

Nofret smiled. For indeed it had been a tidy sum of days and nights since she had been near any man that had aroused her to want him again like her young friend here. There were a couple of handsome men in the village that she enjoyed talking to, but no more than that. Here she was still a virgin. Well, sort of.

A wry smile hovered on her lips as she recalled a woman a bit out of luck recently who needed tender healing. She was a belly dancer. Rather than accept her coinage, Nofret had asked her to teach her the fine art of this exotic dance. Readily she accepted and the two had become fast friends over the weeks.

***

As time progressed, she became quite proficient. Then it dawned on her why she wanted to learn. A warmth spread through her at just the thought of how much she would enjoy taunting that great warrior. Again. She glanced back at Asofia, who was staring at her with a puzzled look on her face.

Nofret bit back a laugh. "Go ahead and rest until needed. I am going to start mixing my powders." She turned and got to work. When the fire was ready, the water was brought and the liquid put in the vial. Shortly after, the ritual walk to the queen's chambers commenced.

After she drank and handed it back, the queen spoke, halting their exit. "Healer, just a moment. I must tell you something of urgency. In confidence." The others moved away, turning their backs to them. "Last night was different. He was different. I was different. Today I am different. I hope sense is being made of this."

Nofret smiled up into her eyes, nodding, already aware of what would happen. "Yes, and so it shall be. Remember? I declared it." The queen clasped her hands tightly and they both softly laughed. "Go on then, healer."

Onward into the next day, night and following night, not only did the queen feel altered, but her appearance did indeed take on a distinctive appeal that had many glancing in her direction. Now she did indeed have that decided glow of a woman that held a child growing inside her womb.

Life was good in the healer's world.

The soldier was more content than ever before.

As the day of departure dawned bright, hot and clear, Nofret packed up her carpet bag and left toward the queen's quarters. Immediately she entered, passing her sage, who halted and grabbed both her hands.

"You are indeed a gifted healer. For you have done that which no other has. Now go ahead in. She is excitedly awaiting your arrival."

The queen's eyes were pooling as Nofret swiftly eliminated the short distance between them. Taking one palm and placing it on her abdomen, a quivering smile appeared upon this lady of royalty's lips. Nofret raised her hand up from her stomach and touched one tear before it fell to their feet.

"Nothing but joy, my queen. I see nothing but joy. As well as a strong, healthy son. He will bear the name and resemblance of your husband, our king. But your true beauty will shine in his eyes always and his heart will know the pure, true love of you both. He will be a commanding and fair ruler. If ever you are in need of my services, please send word. I shall come as quickly as possible."

"Wait just a moment longer. I know they prepare for your departure down at the boats." The queen drew off a table a small silk parcel and unwrapped it. It was a beautifully forged gold and silver cat, sitting upright with a basket of papyrus reeds popping out of the top.

"Oh, this is lovely. I shall put it on now." The healer removed the tie over her shoulder, looped it through the brooch and tied it back. Indeed, it held an important meaning which the healer would not recall until much later. In fact, several lifetimes later.

"It is just as special as you are, Nofret Qalhata, the healer." Her face suddenly turned stern, eyes drawn as if she was angry. Nofret stepped slightly back, not understanding this mood swing as apprehension weaved through her gut.

The queen stepped closer. "Now you must listen and listen well. If I never give this to you again, it means the gods have smiled on us all. At last. Go. I will be in touch soon. You will find the same boat will take you back down the Nile. There is a surprise awaiting you, perhaps more than one. May the heavens always smile upon you, healer, as they smile upon me."

Nofret was temporarily paralyzed. Her mind wove between the here and now and a vision of a handsome man dressed in strange clothes sporting a tall hat of some kind on his head. His voice held an accent she was not familiar with and he seemed to be standing directly in front of the queen.

"Come home. I need you to come home." was all she heard as the vision evaporated.

The queen's gaze questioned her. "Are you okay?"

"Yes. Yes, I am," she lied. "I saw a wonderful glimpse of your future. It is filled with bounty." She nodded, bowing slightly, then walked out of the chambers. But the strange man's words resonated inside her brain. Her heart. Something was stirring there that she just did not understand. Had she been hallucinating? Inhaled too much of the liquid in the vial?

Her eyes drifted towards Meliah carrying the carpet bag. Without distractions on the trip back, she would have time to filter out exactly what her intended message truly meant.

"It is a wonderful day for your return, healer."

She glanced down the few remaining marble steps towards the plank, taking the bag. "Indeed, it is. Meliah, thank you for all your help. I am sure our paths will cross again. Until then, be well."

The sun was bright, too bright, she thought, raising a hand to shield her eyes. Then she walked straight into a wall of iron.

Chapter Four

"Oh." The bag dropped as her hands slid up a walled chest of muscular strength. She let out a gasp. It was someone she knew quite well. He leaned down, picking the bag up with one hand while clasping her petite one in his other. Moving slowly for one so tall, he escorted his lovely guest the rest of the way up the plank onto the ship as the clouds continued to shroud the sun above.

It was him.

Damn, what the hell was he doing here? Did he not have an army to train, someone to irritate or something to burn?

"Healer No fret."

Why did he bother? Why did he not just throw her down on the ship's deck and have his way with her in front of these men? Why did she feel such strong stirrings radiate throughout her being in proximity to this guy? Sure, he was handsome as sin. Sin being the key word here. She did not want to provoke him at all. But no matter how hard she tried to dislodge her hand from his iron grasp, he would not accommodate.

"General Aiemapt." The deep, dark urge to kick him in the balls, or give him a good, hearty shove backward and have his ass land in the shallows was overtaking common reasoning. But she refrained and it was a tough task to fulfill. They walked side by side as she dropped down into what was now that familiar chair adhered to the deck. As the plank was removed and the shore began to recede, her hopes of ignoring him went down the river along with the current. Fast as hell.

He left her and was engaged with someone, but her eyes watched him like a hawk, mind wandering. There had been many times of late when their paths had crossed. Especially recently when she had been visiting a sage in the village near the palace. He'd shown up when she was heading out on her camel. Oh, how his eyes had burned into her very soul. A gruff voice verbally warned her that chasing off by herself could prove to be detrimental. She had lowered her eyes, thanked him, and then moved on. But in fact, she had wanted him to assist. Give protection. A few extra moments in his company. Damn. That arrogant bastard had launched an attack on her heart and was winning.

Eyes seductively drifting closed, head lifting toward the warm breeze, a not-too-subtle emotion was generating from the inside out. It caused scandalous feelings where her skin was exposed.

His eyes devoured her and she could feel it.

"Trying to ignore me this time won't work, healer. You are now my captive. Unless you can walk on water, as I've heard claimed, then how about we start with something simple. Would you like a drink?"

A smile hovered as a soft sigh escaped her lips. His hand extended, producing a goblet of wine.

"Yes, thank you. I will go easy on this, though. Every time I drink it strange things occur."

Their eyes locked. Seconds passed by. She did not even know if her lungs were working.

"You were successful with the queen?"

"I'm not sure I'm at liberty to discuss that with anyone. No disrespect to you, General."

He leaned down, putting one sandal up on the rise beside her chair. Unlike another circumstance when her eyes had refused to wander, this time she had no choice but to allow them to drift up that leg.

"You do not need to fear me. Nor put a wall between us that will surely come down. I know my reputation sparks anger and disgust in many, but I would not wish it to be so with you."

Her heart skipped a beat, lower lip dropping. She'd have to be very careful with this mighty man.

This time.

"Well if you are honest, then so shall I. Your prowess on the battlefield speaks volumes. There is not a man near or far who can beat you. Of that I am sure. But your willingness to burn, pillage and kill using your mighty sword and chariot will be your downfall. You seek to destroy anything and anyone that steps in your way."

"I see you are not fearful for your life, having proclaimed such about me."

She did not flinch, nor feel threatened by him at all right now on her second goblet of wine. "Not one bit."

He laughed. It was hearty. Enveloping her. Bearing charm and arrogance. "Perhaps I am all of those things. But not at the same time. Remember, little one, I follow the orders of my king first and foremost."

"Okay, that may be true. But your journeys have been many and your successes great." She pointed to that glorious sword attached to his belt. "You created that. To many, you are one step away from being a god yourself. Years before you pass on."

"Do not humor me, woman. We know again and again what this is all about. Why don't we just cut to the chase and put all in a right order?"

"You speak of that which I am not clear on. What would you mean to have me say, warrior?"

He was getting pissed off. "But in those that seek to glorify me, I do not cast a glance. There are only a few that truly matter You are one. So here is your chance. I cannot rip you in two and cast you out to the Nile gods, as you are under the protection of the queen. What do you think of me, really? I will not have you hold anything back now so we can avoid a repeat. I want to know."

She shrugged, trying, as with the queen, to fathom

what exactly he was saying. But he stood fast, not moving an inch, awaiting a reply. His eyes would see right through to her soul if she attempted a lie. Her hand went up, pleading.

"I have no wish to anger. Are you so very sure you want to hear my words? I am by nature a healer, not a vengeful person."

His turn to shrug, anger giving way to apparent annoyance and frustration.

"It is not clear to me if you will tolerate my company, or allow it out of true feelings. Perhaps I came upon your good nature for a reason. As you are here to heal me in different ways than the queen."

There was a pause while neither spoke. Then it occurred again. The wind was warm on her body but it was not filling the sails above. Her eyes fluttered shut as her fingers clutched tightly to the chair.

"Nofret?" He was down on both knees, hands cupping her cheeks as she opened her eyes.

"I am afraid of you. I've been lying to myself. You are more potent than any potion I could make. I think even from the grave you would haunt my heart and perhaps you have done so."

His hands stopped. He did not look at anyone but her. "I would never hurt you, love; it will be you that does it to me."

Her hands went over his. "I believe I know and I am very sorry." She refrained from adding that another from the heavens or the grave was seeking her out as well.

He stood, refilling her goblet as her breathing returned to normal at last. Those visions finally evaporated. "Will you be riding with me to the village?"

He nodded. "I have received word that there is one close to your own who wishes to speak with me. I used that as my excuse to be with you on this return. Also, it suits me to go there rather than hold this particular conversation inside the barracks or at the palace."

"Are you testing me?"

"I have no need. It is not I that does not trust. It is you. But it won't be long now. At last, I feel the tides shifting."

She eyed him skeptically. "You know more than you are telling me, Rano, and I do not like it."

He leaned close, too close.

She wondered why he had not kissed her yet.

"Ah, I see that look in your eyes. It's coming soon, woman, so you best prepare. Once I do, there will be no turning back. I leave you now. But I want you to understand one thing. I never quit. This time, Nofret, we will do things my way."

"Why does everyone keep giving me..." Her words trailed off as he stalked away. "Warnings?"

"Damn," she spoke out softly as he disappeared. "I really need to get back to the sanctuary of my tent so I can put this all together."

Her eyes constantly searched for him. Her mind was convinced that he was a demon in a handsome man's body. She would not want him. No, not even if it took a special potion to stop the thoughts of him that were running through her head.

Yet a searing heat, hot and unstoppable, spread through her lower body as her upper lip broke out in a sweat. She swiped it aside with a finger, resting the other hand on her abdomen. But it increased. Closing her eyes, she felt the pulsating invasion increase, forcing her chin up and her head back onto the cushions. She grasped tightly at her tunic, lower lip dropped, until the feeling finally started to drift away. *Oh, my God,* she thought, opening her eyes and staring at him across the deck. Yes. He had done that. Just made love with her body from over there. With his powerful mind.

He grinned, resting a strong hand on the railing,

refusing to come closer. How in hell had he done that? But more so, why? That had been extreme torture. Yet somehow pleasurable at the same time. A shudder passed as she lowered her eyes, knowing he had felt it too. Even from where he stood.

Resting back, she allowed the retreating sun to soothe her invaded body and mind and drifted off into a deep sleep.

He lifted her up as if she was a sack of feathers, while she tucked her head under his chin. Her hand wound its way up behind his strong neck, feeling the warmth there as a sigh escaped her lips.

She felt him set her down on the cushions, cover her body with a rough blanket and speak quietly to someone close to them. "You let her sleep. But when she wakes, make sure you have food and drink ready. She did not have much today."

Nofret listened to his retreating footsteps, wondering if he was going to the helm to be with the captain. Then she fell into a deep sleep until stirred by loud voices. Eyes opening slightly, she watched a hand appear, tying back the draping. Moving onto a side and sitting up, she felt a bit dazed while glancing into the eyes of the awaiting servant.

"I must have been quite tired last night. I have no recollection of getting up from the deck chair and walking in here. Strange." It was a small fib and she knew it, but she had to make sure it had not been a dream with Rano.

"You did not. It was the General that carried you in his own arms. It was with great care he decided to not wake you as you were sleeping so sound."

"Oh."

"Here is your food and drink. You must be hungry. When through, I will remove it. Today we dock and you move onward into your journey."

As Nofret ate, she glanced quickly at the retreating

back of the servant. Those last two words echoed around inside her head. *Your journey.* Who was she? Someone from long ago or into the future? Upon closer scrutiny, she realized it was a woman from a place that appeared in thoughts and dreams from a distant land. A modern land of cars and trains. Yes, it was that same attendant from the Exeter BritRail Station.

Then he came into view, walking closer as she squinted, making out his shape through the flimsy curtains. The acute disappointment was clear when he did not halt. Rather, he continued along. Nofred shook her head and finished the food before stepping outside and into the bright daylight. Instead of going to that chair, she continued along toward the rear of the ship.

Stopping, she reached up and removed the gold rope from her hair, running fingers through it as waves of tingles weaved up from her toes, prickling her skin along its journey.

He took the cord from her hand while taking in his own a thick mass of her wavy hair. Weaving the band around its silkiness, Rano secured her hair at the bottom.

A pulsating need ran rampantly through her as his rough hands gently caressed her neck.

"You slept well. Did you eat?"

Her voice was faintly soft, filled with unchecked emotion. "Yes. I understand you carried me last night. Thank you." She had wanted to chastise him for not waking her, but those words remained dormant.

"We will make land later. Would you like to stretch your legs and come up with me to the first oarsman? He is steering us. Perhaps you may like to give it a try?"

"Won't that upset him? I don't know if we should ask."

"It's only for a few minutes so you can feel how powerful the boat is. I already inquired while you slept and he agreed if the timing was right that he would allow it."

"You mean most of the men are below deck preparing for our arrival?" She grinned up into those penetratingly dark blue eyes. When had they become blue, anyway? Last she remembered they were black orbs of destruction.

He took her by the hand, grinning. "You have things figured out before they become a fact. Yes. You are correct. Do you want to take this opportunity?" But they were already walking hand in hand toward the first oarsman before she realized what had occurred.

"Stand here and hold the tiller exactly as I do, with one hand over the other. Keep your eyes focused toward the front statue of Anuket. That will keep the ship toward the middle of the river where the water is deepest."

She placed her hands on the tiller exactly as he instructed. A strong tug from the current pulled against the sails and caused her to lose her footing. Rano steadied her, hands on her hips.

She did not care that he took such liberty. This was fantastic. The gold cord in her hair undid itself, releasing up into the air as her hair took to the breeze. He caught it just before it went airborne while keeping her firmly footed.

"You would make a good sailor, healer. How does it feel?"

"Strong, Rano. I can't believe how much it wants to pull against me. This is amazing." She was laughing, trying to stay upright while feeling his hands tightly against her hips. Then the captain was back, taking the tiller from her hands and nodding that it was time for them to move along.

She skirted quickly around as he laughed at the burst of energy. "That was so wonderful. How did you know that I would like that so much?"

He placed both of his hands over hers and lowered her right one over his heart so she could feel the beat of it.

That worked.

Her eyes lowered, as did his lips, onto her plush soft

ones.

He did not plunder or punish or command. Instead, he let her take the lead as their tongues touched. She rose on her tiptoes as their bodies melded together, a soft moan escaping from her into his mouth.

Settling her heels back down on the deck, he swiftly swung her around, taking her hand. "I will leave you here and go prepare my things for our land journey."

She did not sit on the chair. Instead, she chose to stand and watch him walk away. At the railing she pulled her flowing hair to one side, holding on to it and wondering exactly when it had come undone. "I guess you have it now, don't you?" she whispered out over the Nile.

He came back up, setting his bag down, but did not move over toward her. As the ropes were being thrown to men ashore, she walked back to her bag. She reached down just as he did and their hands touched. Eyes locked, his roguish smile weaved warmth around her heart.

"You are too powerful for me, mercenary."

"No, you have that all wrong. It is you that is too powerful for even a great warrior like me to resist."

Her eyes glazed over. The shouting voices receded and as if in a trance, she leaned in and kissed him again. Then moved slightly back.

His smile grew.

She walked slowly down the plank, knowing he was directly behind. They moved away from the bank and up towards the awaiting camels. His hand suddenly halted her progress. She glanced up at him, her eyes questioning.

"This way. I brought along a chariot with us. The men assemble it now. I thought you may like to ride in one to see how fast they move through the desert in comparison to the camels."

She grinned, not being able to hold it back. Yes, she liked to try new things and this contraption was all the talk. They had used it in several conquests in Ethiopia and word of its success had spread like dry reeds on fire.

He helped her up and put the bags between them as he took up the reins and steadied them off. It was bumpy and fast at first and she slid into him. Quickly he stabilized them both with his right hand. "It is like being on board the ship with the ebb and flow from the waves. Think of it that way. You have no trouble on the seas. Your legs need to adjust. That's all."

"I like this. I have heard about them from villagers and even saw drawings being carved on some of the caves I've visited."

"Yes, they are not what any other army has. Egyptian advancement is far superior to all others."

"I agree with you. That, along with the sword and speed of the horses, well, you could run right through all enemies."

"That's the idea. Supremacy."

"But how long in this heat can those animals go without water? Surely not as dependable as a camel."

"For true your words are accurate. The camel is used for longer journeys when we do not know where our enemy is. These are used for the final battle when the horses are freshly watered, fed and rested. We plan ahead. Our routes are known in advance. We send a group of men in a water caravan and they place the jugs several cords apart. They submerge them into the sand where only tops are seen. We know from our shared maps where these locations are along our routes. It has proven to be very successful."

"You are giving away your battle secrets, Rano." Her mood had lifted. The way he dealt with people was not her concern. But at least like this, they were equals and she could move those ugly things he was said to have done to a place in her mind where she'd not resurrect them. This time.

"I will share a truth with you. It really was my

choice to have the camels unavailable. I wanted to have you to myself."

She remained calm.

"I'd like to know why you wish to keep a distance between us. Or, if that has changed. If it has not, then I want to know why your eyes and kiss say something completely different than your words."

Her cheeks flushed. "I have no wish to harm you with words that I cannot back up any longer."

"But there is more. Something lurking in a dark area of your mind. Ask me. There can never be any barriers between us, Nofret. Now nor in the netherworld."

She hesitated. "All right. But this is not easy. Why did you have to slaughter all the Semites? I heard even the children and women were not spared from your wrath."

"That is not an accurate statement. The men, yes, were slaughtered. Especially those that chose to run instead of halting. But we did go in with a delegate from the Pharaoh asking them if they preferred exile. To work for him or choose death. They chose death. We did give them a choice."

She was silent for a few minutes as the rocky hills up ahead signaled they were fast approaching her village. "What happened to those that did not fight?"

He shifted the reins, pulling them back, slowing their progress. "They are encamped with all their belongings in a segregated area outside of the walls of the palace. They will set up trade markets, work and earn a good living. Under the rule of Thutmose III."

"What was done with the bodies? Left in desert sand to be eaten by the ravens?"

"You have heard grave stories, have you not? No. We did leave them there while we searched the hillsides and areas around their encampment and villages, making sure we took care of everything. Then their own people, who we knew were still in hiding but were left unharmed, went back to bury them properly. They were by then under our protection. We had guards observing. We even allowed those chosen few to leave unharmed to a new location."

Her heart was softening as his rugged, muscular, tanned arm brushed up against her bare one. "I have nothing else to say."

"Oh yes, you do. I know there is more. Speak of it now before time runs out for us on this day."

She hesitated. How the hell was she to explain to him about visions of another whom she was not sure was a demon or dream? About knowing things in a time that did not exist from sages and scribes? He surely would think her crazy. Hell, she thought, it could be true. Perhaps she was going crazy.

"Nothing."

Screeches of delight from the children lifted towards them as they came running at top speed. He slowed the horses down to a trot. "I don't want you to think any more or less of me. But I will share this with you. I am not a gentleman. I am a soldier. A mercenary. Hired by Pharaoh to come and train his expanding legions to conquer. But I would never hurt you or those you care for. When you come to me, there would be no other. With that, I promise. I am always a man of my word."

He stopped close to a large group of people. Young and old alike circled the chariot as two buckets of water were brought over for the horses and placed beneath them so they could drink.

"Your people are quick-witted and thoughtful."

"Yes, they are. I have perhaps wronged you, mercenary. I think more than once. Yet I am thankful you brought me back so we could talk." There was a double meaning to that which she did not realize right away. He got down, taking her bag in one hand and hers in the other until her sandals were back on the sand. The horses finished and were standing at bay.

"Healer, our paths will cross again and quite soon. Mark my words, you will not be able to dismiss what is between us from now to then. What has happened and what will." The back of his rough hand smoothed over her soft cheek, lifting her chin up so their eyes locked. "There is no place you will be able to hide from me, Nofret, until this is resolved."

When his hand dropped, she grabbed for it, momentarily holding on, and then let it go. Smiling, she stepped aside, the bag now in hand. Her eyes never left his as he climbed back on the chariot. Pulling sharply on the reins, he spun the horses around and rode tall and proud out of her village.

"That was quite an entrance."

She smiled. "How is he, Dahlia? I am anxious to see him."

"His fever broke late this morning and he's resting soundly. He's able to get more liquids in him and I gave him another dose at mid-day. Here, let me take your bag."

They walked through the village, where voices could be heard discussing who had brought the healer back. She grinned, letting the flap down and inhaling the scent of sandalwood. "It is always good to leave. Better yet to come back. I appreciate it much more when I do."

"So, what did the queen want? Can you tell me? I swear I will not breathe a word of it to another living soul."

She shook her head, letting the backside of her hand touch his now cool brow. "No, but perhaps a word of what happened will reach us in a few months. I suspect so. It should be good news."

"Ah, I get it. Since she tried to conceive and lost the child called Amenemhat, successor to the throne. I think that's what you are talking about without committing any words to it."

She grinned. "It won't work. Now, I'm going to bathe down at the pool. Want to come with me? When I come back, I'll assess him and see what is next. He will need a shave as soon as he's well enough to sit up and realizes what we are doing. Can't try it now. If he suddenly moves, his throat could well be sliced before he even knows he has survived."

They laughed and Dahlia decided to join her in the water.

"The coolness of this pool always feels soothing. Tell me what you know. You mentioned it in your scroll."

"At first it was just mumblings of a sick man. Then, there was one name he repeated several times. I believe he was asking for someone very important. Someone he knows well. A woman, I think. But I have never heard a name like that before. It was Samantha."

Stunned, Nofret felt her heart stop beating for a split second.

"He did? Was there more?" She submerged quickly, rinsing her hair of goat's milk and honey wash. "Was his accent from afar? A land we are not familiar with?"

Dahlia shook her head. "No, it is Egyptian. Who do you think he is?"

"Well, we will find out. That is a strange name indeed. I wonder what land that hails from."

"It can't be any place around here, I think."

"Anything else transpire while I was away?"

"No, all is well. We heard about the massacre of the Semite nation."

"If word of what I am about to say gets out, I could be labeled a traitor. I do not agree with the tactics of king and warrior. But I had it from Rano himself that they fought a fierce battle. They were outmatched by the charioteers with their mighty swords." She knew Dahlia was not prone to gossip. But she had to be careful all the same.

"So he happened to be your escort back. Why was that? Surely you must see, as we all do, that he means to have you. You are very fortunate, Nofret, that he has not just taken you as he has other women."

"Not yet, anyway. I have no notion to allow it either. I am now under the queen's protection. If all goes well, he will not want to cross those boundaries with her." She grinned. "I have just realized that. He has to tread carefully with me." She smiled, wondering who was going to protect him from her. She had been quite bold and brazen with him on the ship and the journey into her village.

"That puts you in a better spot with him if he does try anything. I think I'm through here. My skin is shriveling. I will go and replenish the herbs and oils and have food and drink brought to you soon."

"Thanks, Dahlia. I won't be much longer." Resting her head back, his parting comment resonated through her mind as she whispered, "Maybe I shall steal your heart, great mercenary. You had better be on guard at all times." Feeling smug, she rose, dried off and dressed, taking the supplies inside the tent. Setting them down, she moved back and lifted one flap to ventilate the interior.

Although large, today it felt decidedly small with this patient in it. As she stood glancing down at him, he mumbled something. Then he swiftly turned his head toward her. Suddenly bolting upright, he sat straight, staring at her, eyes boring into her soul. She eyed him suspiciously, not quite sure what he was up to.

She took one step back. "You are feeling better. We had thought you for dead. Mind you to say what your name is? I am the village healer, No fret."

She sat down on the cushions next to him and was mesmerized at how his eyes swept right through her. "Have we met before?" He sat up further, leaning close. "No, we have not. I am indeed in your debt and should not trespass on your kindness any further." He tried to get up and then winced, sitting back down.

She laughed. Already it was apparent he was another stubborn man. Did she need two? "It's not the time for you to go. The wounds are not healed. Perhaps in a few more days. Although you have taken to our treatments nicely."

A needed breath was taken. By them both.

"Where is your village? How is it you happened to be brought here? The old man that came in with you cannot speak. Only sign. We were hoping you would recover so more details could be obtained."

"I was in the Lowers moving with a caravan of goods when we were accosted by desert bandits. They must have thought me dead, for surely they would have finished me off if they knew I was still breathing."

"Who is the old man? He dragged you in on the backside of a mule. He clearly was nearly dead on his own feet and quite sick. We have nursed him back to health by another here in the village. He did not need remedies. Only food, rest and time. Shall I have him brought to you?"

"Who was nearly dead? The mule or the man?"

She had to laugh at that. "The man. Do you want him brought in?"

"Yes. If you would. Or I could go to him when I am stronger."

She straightened. "No need. I will see to that now. I will have a platter of food and drink brought in for you both and will allow plenty of time for a reunion."

Without warning, breathing became an issue. Inexplicably, it was apparent she needed to get the hell out of this tent and away from those penetrating eyes. Her brain was trying desperately to give her a message. A message she simply refused to allow.

"I'll return later. Someone else will show your friend in."

Silence permeated around them. Shaking her head, Nofret turned and left the tent. Quickly she found an older man. "Will you please go and get the other one and show him into the invalid's tent? I must attend to a pressing matter."

"Yes, healer. Right away."

"Thank you. No need to stay. They need to converse with privacy."

He looked at her skeptically and went to do as bid.

***

When his friend walked in using a cane, Jared tried again to rise. He glanced around, dropping the tent flap, knowing they were secure for now. "No, my son. Stay put and gather up your strength. We have work to do." He stopped talking just before their meal was brought and continued when they were again alone.

"How are you feeling?"

"Gaining strength. Her treatments are potent."

"That they are. You were so very close to death. I did not think I would see you sitting up. Let alone the two of us having a conversation."

"How did you find that mule and get me here? You are, after all, a very old man, Jacob. By the way, none of them believe you can speak. Until we leave, you had better continue that ruse. This is not the time for us to be brought under suspicion."

They both glanced over at the opening. "It was roaming up near one of the caves. I had to chase the beast down. You can only imagine the discussion I had to have when I finally caught it. I felt like a wild-west cowboy, for heaven's sake. Roping then tugging it under dire protest until it finally figured out who was the boss. But joking aside, I did what I had to do. You were lying there dying, my friend."

He stopped, head turning toward faint voices and then continued as they faded. "It was even harder to lift you onto it. But I had to. I hid us when the army came back with the captives to bury our dead. They lie out there in marked graves. They allowed a decent burial."

"It was to be an equal fight. How truly little we knew about their charioteers and those swords. But we did engage hard. Did many survive?"

"Out on the battlefield, only you. Others in the caves ran and were soon caught and captured. The ones that did surrender are outside the city under custody, working for the Pharaoh in the markets and fields."

"We have to come up with a plan. Give me a few more days and I'll have it. Is the mule still around?"

"Yes, she is well enough now to travel, having been well fed and watered. What about the healer?"

"You know about her? Did I talk in my delirium?"

He nodded. "Yes. You love her. I will help you get back to her. You should not have reached out when she was disappearing. That is the very reason I was brought here. Then spared in battle. But, my friend, our work will not be easy. You still have choices to make. The wind needs to blow in a different direction than in both our pasts. I have seen a glimmer of hope this time. Together, we need to see this through."

Jared sighed, feeling strength return after eating the food. "Yes. I will take you up on that. Two are better than one, they say, and I know already what challenges come before us. Old man, we have to succeed this time."

"I will not argue with you on that score. Quiet now, I hear footsteps fast approaching. I had better go."

Jacob rose, passing Nofret while exiting the tent. Their eyes locked momentarily as he smiled at her as if he knew something.

***

Nofret was about to turn around and demand he give her answers, but then thought better of it and continued inside the tent.

"He did not need to leave. I was coming to just check if you two required anything. I see you ate well. That is good. Your strength will soon return. Now you just need time to fully recover."

He leaned back against the rough blankets, eyelids half closed. "Thank you, healer. I will rest now. Feel free to do whatever is needed in here. The noise will not bother me."

She smiled. Two handsome men in one day being nice. Surely all was well in Egypt on this fine day. Or all hell was about to break loose.

As she mixed up new remedies, restocked the jars and put the lids on, another beastly scorpion pissed her off. Shuffling it away with the end of a reed broom, she lowered the tent flap and ushered him out with a hearty bout of swearing.

"You are probably more danger to him than he is to you."

She laughed. "Those damn animals are a nuisance. I have yet to find one good thing that they are here for."

"You know, that's a good point. Unlike the snake or scarab."

"Sometimes I wonder about them as well. I do not like anything that can crawl around me."

"Seems ironic that you are in such a climate, then."

She turned. "Do you have some kind of a message for me?"

That halted his next random comment in mid-stream.

"Why do you ask that? We do not know each other."

She turned back away from him, placing the last jar up on a wooden box. "Sorry. Don't know why I just blurted that. Are you in need of anything else before I bed down for the evening?"

"No, I am fine."

She checked her bedding one more time and slid in, snuffing out the candles. During the night, she was the one that tossed and turned. In her deepest sleep, she uttered just one word.

Adam.

***

He was watching her, eyes raking over her darkened form while he stood over her. Stopping abruptly, just before leaning down and taking her in his arms, he silently cursed towards the heavens and laid down on his blankets.

"Damn, this is not going to be easy for either of us. But this time, love, the struggle will be worth it. You just don't know it yet."

Chapter Five

"Do you want to bathe and take fresh clothes before we load your mule up and send you both toward your destination? I think your friend agreed. Well, he nodded as much. Besides, well, how can I put this delicately and not offend? You both could use one. Anyway, I have a question and I hope you don't mind my curiosity. Where are you two actually headed?"

"Towards Memphis to join others. I'd appreciate your assistance. I am not offended, healer. I do not believe my clothes will hold together if we do wash them. They are close to rags at this point. I don't want to look like a bandit as we enter the city." Jared glanced down at his clothing, knowing they needed to be replaced.

"Go ahead then down to the pool. I will make sure fresh garments are brought. When you are through, one of the ladies will bring you up. Look." Nofret pointed over his shoulder. "I see your friend is already there."

He left and walked on, noticing that it was not the first time today something odd was occurring inside his gut. It was time to move on. But he had one thing he wanted to do before they walked out of here. Down at the pool he allowed the soft enticing hands of two beautiful women to disrobe him, wash his body and dry him off.

Then they dressed him in a long tunic belted with a handsomely woven leather cord. Its status immediately alerted all who took notice that it was designated to the middle-class. Good. With a haircut and the long, dusty old beard shaved off, he smoothed his hand over a clean-shaven face, satisfied.

He glanced over toward Jacob, belting out a laugh. "Go easy on him, ladies. He is old! I need him as healthy as he can be along on our journey to follow. He has a big job to perform, pulling the mule."

They giggled as he was dressed, feet oiled and sandals put back on.

"You can't take this from me. It could be several days that I am stuck in your company and they are ten thousand times prettier." Jacob glanced around as they moved ahead of the women out of earshot.

"Agreed, old soul. Now come along. We have to set out and I have one last pressing detail to take care of."

The women caught up. "Ladies, we are very grateful." He bowed, placing his right hand over his heart. "If we ever return, we will repay your kindness." He let those words trail off, knowing by the brightness in their eyes they fully understood.

They climbed back up the rocky path alone as the women went a different direction.

"She won't recognize you."

He ignored the comment, taking the reins of the pack mule and surveying the area. There she was, picking up two sun-dried sage brushes. She was clutching them tightly in one hand and reaching for a third when his strong mind willed her to look his way.

She did.

***

Dahlia was saying something as Nofret's eyes locked with his. The ground beneath her feet trembled, branches of the remaining sage crushed beneath a tightening grasp. Her lower lip opened, eyes raking him head to toe. Twice. At Dahlia's curious look, Nofret shoved the brush into her hands and began a slow, arduous walk towards him.

She did not know why. But she stopped short of actually reaching him. Oh, but she did know why. She was afraid if she wove her hands up through his hair and found the indent she had felt in her dreams, she'd know.

Somehow, the universe was testing her. A distant face from a distant time.

She shook her head, causing her hair to spill out of the woven band. Now she could tell by the look in those eyes that he was sorely tested. His fingers flinched as she imagined them reaching out and touching one of her unruly curls.

"Jared Malik, you look very different. Almost like someone I thought I may know. But it cannot be. He does not live around these parts."

"Who was that?" He stepped closer, taking both her hands in his. Glancing down at them, she let them rest there as tingles heightened.

"I cannot say. I do not remember. It was a different time in my life. Damn, you have unnerved me. A stranger from the desert whom I brought back to life."

He leaned down, kissed both palms, released them, and stood back. "When it is clear, find me. I am most curious. You will know where that will be when the time arises."

She stepped back, perplexed at his boldly spoken words. With great relief, she saw that Dahlia was now at her side. Mule in tow, the two men set off out of the village toward their next destination with no backward glance. Both women stood rooted to spot and watched them leave.

"Healer, there are times when we block things that have happened to make our life more manageable. Then, there are times when it hits us like the sting of a scorpion from the desert. That is when we can no longer escape it."

Stunning her, Dahlia's words of wisdom penetrated fast into her confused mind. She was unable to halt them and the result hit its mark. It was as if Nofret was in the middle of a blinding desert storm. When it finally moved on, the only thing remaining was a hole where she had been.

She shook.

"You are wiser than your years, my friend. Go back to collecting brush for me. I require a moment to gather my thoughts."

In a daze, walking along a little-used path, she left the village. High above, there was a special location she used for intense meditation and reflection. It overlooked the Nile and desert beyond. The view itself provided the perfect backdrop for thought-provoking memories.

For Nofret, it was a highly powerful, spiritual place.

Sitting, legs folded, eyes lowered, she began softly chanting in prayer to the angels above, asking for guidance. Something. Any sign that would help her understand what was going on all around her now. Rano, Malik, the mute and what the village sage had told her.

As her own internal chatter stopped, a soft voice grew stronger. More explicit. High above, a raven's screech seemed to put the exclamation point at the end of all the visions dancing around in front of her eyes.

"Oh, shit!"

She rose, running down the path around the other side of the village to look for them. They were nowhere in sight. She spun in horror. How could she not have known him dead on the spot? For all that was holy in the heavens, she had let him slip off into the approaching night! "Oh, my God." She fell to her knees, lifting the cooling sand as it sifted through opened fingers. "I screwed it up."

Yes, it was Jared Malik, Prince of the Semite chieftains. But it was also Adam. Lord Adam Griffin. He had not let go of her hand quick enough at the Luxor Museum. "Oh, my God," she repeated over and over, yelling skywards as more memories flourished. Lowering her head to her hands and bending at the waist, she let it all come, unable to suspend it.

"What have I done?"

With strong, purposeful strides, she walked back into the village and right into Dahlia's tent. "You knew."

Dahlia nodded, patting the cushion next to her. "Yes, and I had to keep silent while you figured it out or you would have thought I was mixing the wrong herbs on purpose again."

"What am I to do now? I could not see them. I do not know what way they took."

"You will not do anything. It will be done for you. You will have choices to make. That is why you are back here again. This time, someone else is in control and has intervened, enabling what several of us hope will be a successful outcome."

"Choices between him and Rano?"

"Yes, and they will not be as easy as you think."

"I thought I could not do that. Come back and repeat as that could alter history. Isn't that against the sacred rules of passages?"

"With you, Sam, nothing is as it seems, is it? You are different. Do not be afraid. Trespass where you have been told not to go. This is not your first 'repeat' here. You just had chosen to ignore all the other times. Suppress it from memory as it suited you. And it seemed to have suited you often."

"Hey, you just said my name from the future. Isn't that dangerous? Or, at a minimum, bad?"

"Yes. It will be the only time you hear me say it. I know all about you. I am not the only one here to help. When you leave the village it will be for a new home. You must remember that you have a haven here if you need it. It is better to sometimes take a deep breath and halt progress before you rush into decisions that may lead you where you do not belong. From here on you will remain Nofret until this passage is concluded. We all hope successfully."

She raised hands to flaming cheeks, tears filling her eyes. "I have mixed feelings about them both. I'm probably not knowing it now, but I am glad he is not here. If he was, I'd make a mistake." Rising, head slumped, she headed toward the tent flaps.

"I will see you tomorrow, healer. Pack your bags, jars and anything else of importance. Use your time wisely to stock up. It is important you gain back full energy. Clarity of thought. Make sure you are of sound mind before leaving."

Trying desperately, Sam let one more thought of Adam stay before clearing it away. Would she have to work through all her other lives before they were truly reunited? *Crap*, she thought, sadness filling her soul. If that was the case, then thousands of years would need to pass before he held her in his arms once again.

Feeling positively miserable, she was aware of a soft emotion spreading through her body. A faint voice followed it and as she listened intently, the message was clear. Finally, a slow, steady smile emerged.

All was not lost.

Back in her tent now, a diversion was in order. She lit the sandalwood paste in a golden plate and sat down with a statue of the Goddess Tawaret, who protected women during pregnancy and childbirth. Raising the incense in front, she blessed this statue and chanted until sure the great goddess would give the queen a healthy, strong son and easy birthing.

Wrapping the statue in silk, she placed it in her carpet bag and set about taking stock of what was needed. Tonight when the moon was full, she'd walk the path and gather. Tomorrow it would be finished as the new day dawned. It would not take long to finish bringing together all that was needed.

Grabbing a basket, she set off out of the tent and through the silent village. Singing locus and chattering sheep were the only sounds her ears met on the walk up to the hilltop. Now full of future remedies, she sat down, glancing up into the heavens just in time to catch a streaming, falling star.

"Back where I come from if you see a shooting star you have to make a wish right away. Or you miss the chance."

She expelled a deep breath as her lids closed.

He took one small hand into his strong one.

"I heard you on the wind calling me back."

"I did."

She set the bundles down and moved in front of him, shifting the tunic sideways, and sat on his crossed legs. She had to know. Then again, she already did. Reaching behind his head, she felt the indent. Then she pulled his lips to her own.

He moved back slightly, leaning his forehead against hers. "I am to take you to Memphis with me. The queen's courier met us along the route. Since I knew the way, I was given two camels and instructions. They took Jacob with them to board the ship and await our arrival. It was by order of your Rano the Mercenary."

"Oh." Lifting off him, she stood, hands on hips. "Why did you let me kiss you? Damn, you are an ass. Even here."

She moved toward the trail, feeling a bit humiliated, but would not in ten thousand years show it.

"Because I could. Because I wanted to know if you still had some passion in your body for me before I bring you to him. If you had not, I would have."

Her nostrils flared, her mind reeling. This was probably why she had not wanted to be fully committed to him in the future. "My guess is this. You are a rogue. Throughout all of history. If I am here to do something of importance with Rano, why are you here? To slip off into the city and have your way with dozens of mistresses? Probably, since you did that where we just came from."

"Stop that shit. I gave them all up once you came around."

"Well, here I may not come around." This time she

meant it.

"Look, it was not my idea to come back. This is all pretty screwed up, if you ask me. Anyway—" He stood, not bothering to take her hand, but he did take the basket. "—until we completely understand why we are both here, we'd better keep our distance. If Rano even sees there is anything between us, he will not think twice about killing me. Healer, I need to know why I've returned. It is not all about you and a coincidence that you took my hand and we both made it across. You were destined to drag me with you and I am at a loss why. I have tried without any luck, but my mind is blocking much of this period. Even some stuff regarding you."

Inhaling sharply, air finally rushing out, she had to admit at being pissed off too. "Okay. I am not going to fight with this right now. I am already packed. We can leave when you wish."

She turned to go as he dropped the basket.

"Fuck it. In case you are between fences, let me just remind you who I really am."

As he pulled her hard against him, she could feel his underlying frustration. The passion between them, between all of the time, flared up. Immensely.

She pulled roughly away. "You have to stop that. If you tell me to keep my distance, then you'd better not do that again. I am not always as strong as you. But right now, you were not strong at all."

***

"*Touché*, mistress." He laughed, enjoying the changing of the guard. "It seems you arrived here with even more gusto than you had with me previously. I can't wait to see what happens next."

"Oh, shut up. Now, where are these transporters of ours? What specifically did the courier's letter say? Do you have it on you? I'm quite sure if it was from the queen herself, that I am the one who should be reading it."

"Yes, it's for you." He chuckled at her arrogant display of superiority. "I have it in my pack down below. The camels will be set to go after sunrise. You already know the route, don't you? A boat will be awaiting us. But worry not another thought my way. Once we arrive in Memphis, I will be joining the army. You may not see me at all."

He was trying to get her goat and she'd not have any of it. "It will be as it is and no more."

He softened as the moon glowed from above, all but melting the silk from her luscious curves. "Maybe we just stay right here, you move in, finally confirming our marriage and we have those twenty children."

She spun around, bursting out laughing. "I certainly will not." But her smile lit the sky.

"Then maybe in our next life, after our last life, that's not related to this one. Oh hell. I will shut up now."

"Yes, please do."

***

As they came back into the camp, she left him without another word and spent a few minutes packing up the last needed items. A small batch of flowers could be gathered upon their exit from camp. He would have to stop and that was that. Lying down, she felt the need to speak with Dahlia one last time. Rolling over, she hastily wrote a quick scroll, tied twine around it and left it beside the rug. She'd see it when she came in tomorrow.

Curious, crawling on hands and knees, Nofret flipped one flap partially back a few inches and peered outside. He was sleeping on a carpet just a few yards away. Both camels were sitting down in the sand, eyes closed and making some unusual grunting noises. Or was that him, snoring? Dropping it back down, she stood, laughing all the way back to her cushions at what she had just done. Perhaps it had not been to spy on him, but to make sure he was indeed there.

***

Jared's eyes went from slits to closed as he smiled. He'd seen what that chit was about. But quickly it was replaced by a frown, arms tightening across his chest. Rano. What was to be done about him? He knew part of the story from her before this happened. What was the rest? Was he here to protect her? Lead her like a lamb to slaughter? Bring her back? Make her stay? Or worse of all, let her go for good?

He shook his head. No. He would not let her stay. But if she had to, he would too. It would break all the rules and alter his destiny completely. For her, he would do it. Only for her. Although, perhaps her true destiny did not involve him at all. Just Rano.

"Damn," he muttered, shaking his head. "Enough." He delivered his final thoughts verbally up into to the heavens above in frustration.

As the ravens flew overhead, his eyes fluttered open and he glanced at one that landed in a sagebrush damn close. Those penetrating black orbs mesmerized Malik for a few seconds. "What message do you bring me, my friend? Just an alarm to get up?" He rose, rolling the carpet and securing it on one of the camels. Taking out two flasks, he drew water from the well just as a hand appeared, opening the flap of her tent. Two carpet bags now secured, one in each hand, she walked towards him as his gaze honed in on her face.

"Good morning."

He nodded, settling the bags securely in place. "You need to relay anything to anyone before we head out?"

"No, all taken care of. I am ready." She slid up on the sitting camel as Jared took the ropes and the gentle creature stood. He noticed she seemed well at ease in the whole process.

***

Mounting, they headed out of the village before

anyone else woke. "Did you read the scroll?" Nodding yes, she sipped the cold water inside the flask. "Thank you for filling this. I'd prefer a cup of English breakfast tea filled with organic sugar, cream and a scone from the bakery. Is there any possible way you can fetch that for me and arrive back before we reach the ship?"

He grinned as they continued along side by side. "Yeah, I can just portal there and back before you reach that fork in the path up ahead."

"Oh, thank you. It will make my mood brighter."

He laughed. "Did you not sleep well, healer?"

That was a reminder to refocus her thoughts and curb those comments. *Damn*, she thought, *he is straight to the point this morning*. It would take away their few minutes of fun banter before 'all eyes and ears' would be upon them both.

"I did not. My mind was busy trying to put things together. I guess this is when I just let the wind blow the direction it will and take me along with it. I don't know, Malik. I am really baffled."

"So am I. We won't have much of a chance to engage in conversation like this down the road."

"Are you joining the army so you can be housed closer to where I'll be?"

"And closer to where he will be."

"Ah, a bit jealous, are you? I thought that never happened inside your heart."

"A word of caution here. Just remember all the women I will be around. I should not want for anything should I ask for it."

A sandaled foot shot out but was inches from making the mark.

"Don't say it. Ladies do not speak like that here."

She wove some silk up over her hair and around her ears to keep the dust from coming into her mouth. More than that, to keep it shut. As they approached the outskirts of the port, she saw the familiar sails and crest of the queen's ship awaiting them.

As they arrived, both camels lowered as two soldiers walked, faces stoic and unreadable, over to her. One took her bags and the other motioned with a hand for her to follow toward the plank.

Nofret dared not glance back to see if he was in tow. But from the intense feelings toward her back, it was clear his eyes were on her. Halting a few feet onto the plank, both soldiers stopped behind, one speaking. "Healer, he's waiting."

Oh shit, she thought. One love of her life was behind, ready to board, and the other ahead, looking like he was about to have lunch and dinner in one meal. Shaking her head slightly, determined, Nofret walked into her future and past, combined.

What a sight he was, that commanding figure of her mercenary. Indeed, he was handsome as she pondered if any woman would be able to resist his charms for long. He was at the helm talking with the captain when he caught sight of her.

His strides quick with purpose, Malik passed by them both, nodded, and then continued.

The emotional ties between them she could feel straight to her toes. Not with Rano, but Malik. Yes, he was jealous. Jealous of a man from her past that had loved her perhaps as much as he had throughout the rest of the centuries. They had seen much between them. But now he was not in control. He glanced above, beyond the clouds to the heavens, shook his head in arrogant dismissal of their reasons for him being here, then disappeared to a section no longer viewable by her eyes.

Chapter Six

"Healer Qalhata, welcome back aboard. It seems we have good timing. I just finished my affairs and was advised to hold our sailing for your arrival."

Rano took the two bags, tilting his head to the side for her to pass ahead. As if on queue, the sun suddenly shone down upon Nofret, illuminating her body. Rano's smile increased as he raked her backside head to toe. He housed no doubt she had dressed like this today just to entice him further. *As if proof was needed*, he thought, she glanced back with an inviting smile that matched his own.

They both broke out in laughter, ignoring the looks that came their direction. He leaned down, settling the bags as she suddenly surprised him.

"I am happy to see you again, mercenary."

"What are you up to now, woman? Trying to tighten the strings around my volatile heart further?"

She pushed up onto tiptoes and kissed him quickly. "Could be I am. If that is even possible."

He groaned. "You should be in charge of my army, not I. You by far prove to have more tactical skills."

She giggled. "All women do, Rano. It's just a fact we arrive on the earth with more of it."

Settling back, he motioned the servant over with a tray. Pouring only one goblet, he handed it to her.

"What, not joining me?"

"No, I need to keep my wits about me. Possibly later I will when I can't sleep."

"Well then, let's change the subject. The wind is with us, it is a fair day, let's hope it holds until we arrive. Was your business successful?"

***

Small talk. She needed lots of small talk now to keep from throwing herself at his feet. Yes, she was somewhat aware of a future with Adam, but that was a long, long way off. Right now, things had to be put into perspective. Keeping Malik at a safe distance was necessary. In fact, out of sight out of mind was what she was wishing for.

Her eyes drifted over towards the twosome as Rano's eyes followed.

"Ah, the old man. Yes, he was with your escort so we provided him safe keeping until you joined. If we had not, he would have detained your arrival. He does not speak, it seems. But is proficient in herbs and remedies. Although not as knowledgeable as you. One of my soldiers needed something done of a delicate matter. So he proved his worth straight away to relieve some of his sufferings."

She laughed. "Ah, I see. He was visiting someone in the village and took away more than he paid for."

He joined in, placing a sandaled foot up on a stool, signaling to the captain to prepare for immediate departure.

"Well, he's feeling a lot better now. I suspect he will be right back at it by our next night on land."

"I bet he will. Will you consent and call me Nofret? 'Healer' puts me on a pedestal and I'd prefer not to be on one."

He handed her a small platter of fruits and meats and she ate. "I can do that."

"What will you do with our voyagers when we arrive in Memphis?"

"Jared of Mykonos will join my legion. He's strong and smart. I've already received a needed dispatch about his background. He is of good heritage. I find myself in need of another formidable strategist."

She blinked quickly, staring down into the dark purple wine in her goblet. Jared of Mykonos? He must have come up with a valid story. If Rano had any idea that he was dealing with the chieftain of the expelled nation of Hemite, his blood would boil and he would make quick work of killing him.

She grinned up at him, finding true enjoyment now in both men's maneuvers.

"And the elder, do you have any use of him?"

"Not at all. He can do as he wishes when we arrive. He seems sturdy enough. Just unable to communicate."

"He will come with me then, so it will be settled. I will take him under my guidance. I could use a learned man who can use the herbs. I will discuss him with the queen. I am sure she will allow it. Especially with his skills. I will tell her you consented."

He raised a brow. "As you wish. There is a storm brewing. Our arrival will be sooner than planned. I will have you there before that comes about. The river will rise overnight with strong rain."

"It will be a blessing for the grains and to fill our wells. So tell me, where is your next conquest? Will you be off again as soon as we land?"

"No, not right away. We have preparations to make and reinforced training to take care of. So you see, you will not be able to elude me much longer." He leaned closer, his lips just a few inches from hers as they lowered, anticipating that kiss. "Perhaps we shall become more deeply acquainted, healer. It is time."

Seconds passed.

"I would like that." She lowered her eyes from his heated gaze, feeling a pulsating warmth in her loins. If he could make love to her without touching, oh, what would he do to her when they did?

"Ah, the interest grows, as does the need. I feel what you feel, love. You want us to be alone and naked. I match that. No point in hiding it any longer." He moved closer, sitting on the platform beside her chair. One strong tanned hand rested over her own. "I am to move my quarters closer to the palace when I get back. The Pharaoh has ordered it. There are warnings from trusted advisors that someone may try to kill him or sabotage the army."

"Are you telling me this to test? Surely, this would not be discussed with anyone except whom you have the utmost trust within the upper levels of your liege."

His fingers were weaving through her soft, wavy hair. "I have excellent instincts. You and I have a purpose, little one. Things need to be different between us this time. If it means giving up all the other pleasures I've taken, then I will do it. If it means allowing all the ones you have taken, then so be it."

Her mind wandered a moment. Was that it? Last time he had too many women and she was pissed to not be the only one? No, for some reason that did not seem to be it. Fuck. She needed to remember but was deathly afraid to use her own potions to delve into the darker side of a thought-induced trance to figure it out.

This was a deadly formula from the Book of the Dead. She had tried it once and the ramifications had been awful, practically causing her mind to shut down for nearly three days. It was as if it had cursed her for using it. Body fine, mind paralyzed. There was no way she was going to do that again.

His voice broke into her thoughts at last. "I trust you to not discuss any of what I tell you. It is between a man and a woman. Not healer and mercenary."

She sat back, placing the cup on her lap. Oh, this was a turn of events. She had not expected this man, soldier and sometimes killer, to have such a soft side and affect her inside and out so intensely. "I pledge my silence. You have my word."

He stood, taking one hand into his and placing a kiss there. "I will leave you. I need to speak with my men below deck to prepare for our arrival." He tapped his chest and walked off as her eyes followed every step of his way.

Damn, she thought. This was going to be a big test of strength. He was intriguing. It was just so frustrating only recalling bits at a time. So far it was of little use. She needed more. There was someplace she had turned her nose to near the palace that she was going to visit as soon as time allowed. There, answers would be found.

Everywhere she turned the same words plagued her. Something had to be different this time. Did the lives of many hinge on her? Would he continue to haunt her from the grave for lives to follow if it did not? A cold shiver ran up her spine. No, this time she would not wilt under this enormous pressure.

What about Adam, England, Norway, the Great World War, Anne, Clash and suddenly finding out she had a brother? Would it and all of them simply evaporate from time? Or just from her existence? She was upset. Her insides pulling out, she spewed up to the heavens, "Too many freaking questions unanswered. Can't you do better than all of this shit?"

Jacob, standing quite a few yards away, glanced at her with a smile. There was something in that smile that had her stomping a footed sandal down hard on the deck. No. It was not going to be this time. Period. Samantha Arnesen's courage filled the body of this Egyptian healer.

Rising, she marched over to one of the railings and clutched the wood with white knuckles. A voice penetrated her dark thoughts. "Healer, your bedding is prepared for the night. Would you like to stay here or follow me?"

Nofret's eyes relayed a potent message, but she softened her words, recalling what occurred last time she'd remained on deck. "I will go now. I am tired. Please make sure I am not disturbed. I don't care about the noise out here, but I need privacy."

"As you wish it. Come this way."

Lying down, she moved the blanket, tucking it under her chin as the servant took a place on the opposite side and closed the drapes. "We shall be there by early morning with this wind."

Nofret smiled. "This pitching is not quite as soothing as it was the last time I was on the boat."

"If you need the jar, let me know. I have it ready for either one of us." That caused them both to laugh.

"Good thinking." Nofret rolled to one side and drifted off, listening as long as possible to the voices inside her head. But they did not stop as tossing and turning ensued. Well into the night she suddenly bolted straight up. Glancing at the still sleeping servant, she sighed softly.

Throwing the blanket off and crawling on hands and knees to where the draping split, she peered out. A few were about up at the helm. But the only other noise was the oars' steady rhythm in and out of the water.

"Oh, screw it," she mouthed softly. Then she stood and walked out, venturing toward the closest railing. She gazed up to where the angry storm clouds were gathering, hiding the expansive sparkling galaxies in the sky that she loved to view in the darkness of the night.

"You could not sleep?"

"No. Not really. I thought a bit of air would do me well."

"You care for some company?"

There it was. The moment of truth.

"Yes."

The boat pitched and he grabbed her, pulling her back tightly against his chest while holding the railing with both hands to keep her safe and secure. "What's on your mind that has you unsettled, healer?"

She smiled. Was he ever going to address her informally? "Could be why you have a hard time calling me by my first name, Rano."

He chuckled, the comforting sound reverberating from his chest into her body. "I would call you many things. Should I say them now you may hurt me in your attempt to move away."

She liked this side of him. A bit on the frisky side. "Well, let me be frank then. It appears I do want more of you. There. Said and done." Silently she knew the line had been crossed and she was ready to play at this game.

"It is inevitable, little one." One hand started to roam from holding her around the stomach. It massaged over a hip and then halted briefly before embracing one firm breast. She leaned further into him, head tilting back, wanting to turn straight into those arms and make love with him right here, right now.

"Let me assure you again. Once we are on dry land, you will not get rid of me until the king declares our next conquest and my army and I are commanded to move out."

She was forced to lighten the mood. "Well, you will not be in my wing of the palace. It is a large place. Besides, if you are near the king I assume you will be farther away. Which is much to my delight. I will then have run of the place and can scurry around in the dark corners of the corridors and avoid you. Those that you set out to spy on me will have their hands full. I will give them a good run for it. I know what you are about, Rano. You will have me watched."

His fingers tweaked the taunt peak as a wanting sigh escaped her lips. Increasing this irresistible pleasure further, he applied pressure to her lower abdomen just as she felt his firmness against her backside.

"Oh, mercenary. Yes. It is true I desire you."

"And there will be a time when you will come to me. The pleasure we will have then will be like nothing else you have ever known. Nor I."

Yes. It would be true. She knew it. Until another time well into the future and another man. "A bit cocky, aren't you?"

"Interesting you used that word."

They both broke out laughing. "Oh, stop it."

"You did set yourself up for that one. Unfortunately, I have to attend to a few things. I'm going to attempt this and see how much stubbornness I am met with. Will you come willingly back to your bedding? The waves and the wind are kicking up. I'd prefer to know you are safely tucked back in there and not overboard where no one would know until it was too late."

She turned into his warm strong embrace at last. Yes, it was clear the love they already shared. "I will. I think all this gibberish has tired me out. I will go willingly so you don't throw me over your shoulder like a sack of grain."

"Well now. A small victory for me on this night for sure."

She poked him in the side, letting go of his hand. "Good night, mercenary."

"Sleep well, healer." He dropped the draping, leaving her as she maneuvered back, dropped down, covered up and did indeed regain sleep. It was a peaceful, dreamless sleep that left her completely invigorated the following morning.

***

"Healer, I have your bags ready. They are about to hoist the ropes so we can go ashore."

Nofret was awake and had remained quiet, making a mental good/good list comparing Adam and Rano. Sitting up, she combed through snarly hair. "Thank you. Take those out toward the chair and I will join you in a moment."

Checking the surroundings, she left to join the gathering group. Malik and Jacob were well behind her as Rano slid his hand down an arm and encased her hand.

"I have appointed one of my men to escort you to the palace. There is a rather urgent business matter I must attend to in the village and then with the king."

Good, she thought. *I now have time to put some ideas in motion.*

Strange, though. His next comment made her think he was indeed reading her thoughts. "Don't go off and get into mischievous dealings. I now have those that will hide further into the dark shadows where you will roam and report their findings."

She giggled. "Shut up."

"That is hardly any kind of commitment."

"You are a clever man."

His shoulders shrugged as he released her arm. He nodded to the soldier assigned to her as the plank was placed against the ship. It was as if this protector's eyes bore into her soul with a warning that he would not be so tolerant as his commander would.

She was first off the vessel. Onward they walked as she followed him through the cobbled streets and up the marble steps to her now familiar access into the royal palace. As he drew the doors open, she continued in as he sat the bags down, banged his chest with a fist and left.

She smiled, both at his action and at who was awaiting. "Meliah, Asofia, hello to you both. Are you here to settle me back in?"

They embraced. "No, we are officially assigned to you by our queen. Your quarters have been extended now that you are a palace resident. You still have these three rooms but now two more have been added. Plus a private balcony, gardens, pool and a maid to prepare the meals."

"Well now. That truly is splendid. One of you can unpack the larger bag. I will take care of the smaller one. It houses some delicate items and I wish to inspect them to ensure they fared well during my journey. I have a special gift for the queen. I know it is late now, but am I scheduled to have a visit with her soon?"

"She is already aware of your arrival. As soon as the ship was viewed and you were spotted on land, a dispatched courier brought her the news. Later tomorrow morning we will go and see her after she rises. Her health is good. But she has been feeling a bit strange over the last few days. That is why she requested your urgent return."

Nofret nodded. "That's to be expected. I will reassure her then. You both will have some free time. You probably recall how I like to venture off alone. But this time I return knowing we are now friends. It will be nice to have your help preparing my remedies. I will put my services out for the villagers if they wish to use me. I don't want to be idle."

Now she got down to the real work. "Has that handsome soldier been visiting while I was away?" The threesome all giggled, coming closer, clasping their hands together.

"Yes. He can't decide which of us he likes the best. But we do know he's not visiting any other."

"Well now. Does that mean I may lose you both from living inside the palace soon? I understand if you move your possessions into his quarters, you will officially be his wives."

They laughed as Asofia declared, boldly reminding Nofret suddenly of Anne, "I'm not sure I want to be his wife. I'm young. I may quit our gatherings and let Meliah have him." She poked fun at her friend. "Then I can resume my other pleasures."

"Do you want that, Meliah?"

She smiled coyly. "I would not mind being his wife. But could just one please a man like that? I don't think so. He would be free to take others if he chooses."

As Sam she was laughing inwardly Nofret the Healer was smiling outwardly. Yes, men and women in this era were allowed an open policy on mating, marrying and staying faithful.

There was no cheating here. *Why not let the good times roll?* she thought.

It was a love free-for-all without paperwork, money-hungry lawyers and nasty divorces. How much more simple it was. She grinned, letting go of their hands and opening up the small bag. It was a good thing she had not married Adam. She'd feel a bit of remorse here even though nothing was binding in this period.

That grin expanded two-fold.

"Would you like a pool bath or an indoor one tonight? You are invited to dine in the main area any time you wish. We were asked to tell you. You are not off limits anywhere in the palace by order of the Pharaoh."

"Wonderful. Outside at the bathing pool will do. It is warm and the waters will feel refreshing." She knew the routine even though she was quite able to do this alone. They would hover, assist and then she'd dismiss them for their evening of pleasure. "Well, I am unpacked and you have finished the other bag. Shall we? I'd like to wash off the dust from my trip."

They lathered and oiled her body and hair and then towel-dried her. She was wrapped in a new outfit and belt with matching silver sandals. *Hmmm*, she thought, *not Versace or Louie but sure would do*. Both those designers would cry out to heaven to have such raw materials at their use.

"Thank you, ladies. Come when the queen requests me tomorrow and we shall go there together. Otherwise, you both enjoy your night." She smiled as they parted, walking around a band of soldiers having just come from the corridors of Thutmose III.

Rano stopped, nodding for the others to continue along.

"Heading to dine?"

"Yes. Care to join me?"

"I will." He took her hand in a gesture that was not common in this period. He should have taken her arm. That was two or three times he had done that now. They walked into the great room, where the chatter minimized as Nofret walked by the queen's table and nodded, smiling warmly at her. It was returned by one laden with relief.

"You are a favorite now. Everyone here will want to get closer to the queen's new healer." He sat her down on a pile of cushions and waved for attendance.

"Well, it will pass. I live quietly. I came in here tonight so I could see her. Otherwise, I would have taken food and drink in my quarters. I do not prefer to be in the limelight."

He drew in a brow. "Limelight? What does that mean? I am a learned man, but do not know I've heard that."

"It was a word a passing tradesman used in our village a while ago. According to him, it means one does not like to be in the center of attention from others."

"Where was this tradesman coming from?" He was getting nosy. "I am not sure, since many pass through the village on the way to the Nile. I could be right in saying he was from East Asia since his robe looked like it was from a distant place."

That settled it nicely.

But there was something Nofret needed to know right now. "Did you move your quarters?"

His mouth was full of food and she hid a grin, awaiting his reply.

"Yes. We had just come from the Pharaoh's area having just finished. I have rooms close to his now. So the royal palace has two new residents. You and I."

Oh great, she thought. He'd be under her nose until whoever had threatened Thutmose III this time was caught and executed. "How does your search progress?"

He leaned closer. "It was rumored that suspicion was being housed on that man Jared of Mykonos. But an additional dispatch has arrived confirming what I already know. He is no longer being watched. Did you settle the elder?"

"He is in a guest area until I can speak with Queen

Satiah tomorrow. Surely you do not suspect him? Granted he is older, but surely..."

He held up a hand. "No. He was also listed in the dispatch. He is no harm here. Mykonos has joined my legion and is in training with my men. He has already shown to have superior skills close to mine. So this process will continue until our next campaign. I have placed him under my second-in-command. He has intelligence and I plan to use it. Some of his ideas are more advanced than we are using."

"Isn't that odd that he has superior knowledge?"

He eyed her suspiciously. "What are you saying, woman? That he could be an implant, a spy? Or set here for high treason?"

Her voice shot up. "No, of course not. I guess I am not understanding how his knowledge could be greater than yours."

"You have the mind of a general and the smooth talk of a snake in the Garden of Eden. It is possible no person is here to threaten our king. Perhaps it is just that you are here to threaten me."

"I'm ignoring that. But surely you won't go on that campaign until the person is located and disposed of?"

"I see and hear more now, Nofret. It could have been planted as a rumor to get me into the palace and away from the army while a spy is routed in. This is now merely a precaution. I do not think a threat is posed on Pharaoh at all. Nor do I believe this person has anything to do with Malik and the elder."

She smiled sweetly, as he had used her first name. "How wise of you. So by removing yourself, that person may feel more comfortable and drop their guard down and be exposed. You should have him taken to the priestesses. It is known their charm could work any words from a traitor's lips."

"Or I could send him to you. Perhaps you have a

serum you could give him?"

They both leaned in as his tanned muscular arm heated up her right side, resting possessively against a hip. "Sorry, what did you ask me?"

He leaned in then and kissed her sumptuous lips.

Her hands wove up around his neck, clasping, taking him prisoner completely. As their mouths parted, softly she spoke. "I hope you don't leave too soon."

He stayed close. "Long after the rising of the Nile from heavy rains and when the grain is harvested, then we will be going. As to where I will not say. For you may decide to follow."

She smiled as the musicians began playing. The exotic scents of the scantily-dressed dancers arrived long before their bodies. Dancing seductively around their table, one got bold, leaning over and letting her breasts spill nearly out. With a flicker of a hand, Rano moved them along.

"You insult them by your quick dismissal."

"I will do as I please. They do not hold my attention this night."

There it was again, gruffness. Or was it frustration? Was he trying to make a bold statement to all that were watching? Was this just a show and later on when he retired to his chamber others would be there taking care of his needs?

"Do you dance like that?"

Their eyes locked. That was normally a question not asked by a man of a woman at all. It was just expected she 'knew' how to please him in every way. Women here learned from their mothers and it was passed down for many generations.

"Yes." She was getting as bold as he was.

"I am intrigued by you. Again."

"Yes, I am fully aware."

"I will have you, you know."

She shook her head slightly. "I am aware of that too."

"On top of being a healer, do you also possess the same gifts as the Goddess Maat?"

She giggled. "Truth, balance, morality, justice and can see the future? No. Well perhaps a little of each, yes." That was true. For she was already special, wasn't she? How many here in this room right now were involved in a 'passage' of some kind? That intrigued her. Indeed, she thought as she glanced about the room, she'd never know the answer to that. Perhaps Rano was as well? No. He was a man who needed her for some very special reason and she was here to know why and help. So if that involved being in an intimate relationship, then who was she to scoff at the gods' requests?

His eyes were intently upon her as her mind had wandered. His voice brought Nofret back to the present. "You were distant. What words were taking place in your head?"

"There will be times when a woman will share that. This is not one of them." She reached over and touched his bare forearm. "But it was not dangerously bad, I can assure you."

He put his other hand over hers and let it rest on top. "Of all the forces I've fought against, you will be the toughest, healer." He rose suddenly and she glanced up into his eyes while he extended a hand.

"The hour grows late, Nofret. I will walk you back."

She took that hand. "I bet you already know where they are, don't you? My rooms."

He laughed. "You have a ready answer. So why have you asked it?"

Along their walk she glanced around, noticing changes since she had last been in the palace. "There seem to be more guards posted. Is that because of what has happened?"

"You really don't miss a detail. Yes. We are taking all precautions seriously. But relax. You are free to move about as you wish. Just don't be surprised if you are followed. Under the queen's protection or not."

"Ah, here we are. I hope to see you soon."

She felt bold. It was probably the pungent wine. Two goblets of it.

"Yes."

He pulled her roughly into his arms against that rock-solid chest while grabbing her long, flowing hair in one hand. The other slid up the warm skin of her neck, tilting her chin up as he lowered his lips, claiming hers.

Lifting on tip toes, she did not want to let him go. His kisses were passionate and consuming as all chatter in her brain subsided. He pulled back as her feet lowered down onto the marble floor. "It will not be an easy night to sleep for either of us."

He let her go and she opened up one door, turning toward him. Her body was screaming to grab him by the arm and bring him in, but that hand rested on the frame. He shifted closer, placing his hand over her heart, cupping a firm breast. She swallowed hard as he nodded, gaze not disentangling from her eyes.

"Yes I know," she whispered. Then she closed the door.

***

Slowly he crossed the corridors as his mind demanded an immediate turnabout. Marching back and just taking her. Hell, they both wanted it and knew it. There had never been a time in his life where his mind had to be stronger than his body. Things had to be different this time. Perhaps it was one more venture to the temple? Frustration finally gave way to common sense. Instead, he went back to his own quarters and stayed there. The whole night. Alone.

Chapter Seven

She was roaming the streets outside the palace with her trustworthy guard at hand when she spotted Malik with a herd of women gathered all around. It caught her by total surprise when jealousy and anger did not rise up within her chest.

As if from a distant body, housing a soul that did not know him yet, she looked on with mild amusement. Was this where he started to gather those mistresses? An old saying rang through her head. The apple really did not fall far from the tree. Giggling, she recalled how that was not old as of yet. In fact, not even quoted. Basically, she silently acknowledged what happened in Egypt stayed in Egypt. Okay, she concluded. It worked for her. Winking at him from afar, she waved her shadow to come up beside. He was indeed a handsome bodyguard from the palace assigned by the queen. But she also knew he reported to Rano.

"Do you want to go over and have a jug of wine? I'm just going to look at purchasing some seeds and herbs. Just keep an eye on me so I don't get into trouble."

***

They both shared a grin as he set off, giving her a few megalithic yards of freedom. Hell, he knew this was time off with perks. Each night was a heck of a lot more enjoyable than the last. Finally, he had given up on the women in the village. The ones in the palace really did hold magic in their hands.

As he drank his first goblet down and refilled, she disappeared around the back of a stall, but quickly reemerged with a bunch of some darn thing in her hand. He moved back, leaning comfortably against a stall pole.

"That's Rano's woman, I see. So you were the one chosen to guard her?"

He nodded. "Malik. I see you've taken a handful of my former women. Well, keep them satisfied, I say. There is an abundance at the palace and I am enjoying their delights. So tell me, how are the plans coming?"

"All is in order. Although we may well move out before the queen births. You may find yourself staying behind and missing out on all the action, my friend."

He refilled the goblet. "I don't think so. This is a big campaign and Rano will need all of us on that one. I think I should take the old man aside and show him how to use a sword and spear so he can protect the healer. He seems strong enough. Just looks old."

"Jacob is strong of body and mind, I assure you. His only issue is that he cannot speak. Use him. I've known him quite a while and he's honorable. He'd give his life up for her. He is appreciative of what he learns and already follows her about. Look."

Alioss glanced over. The twosome were nose deep, engaged in some type of an animated conversation. Tucked neatly into his hands were her purchases. "I swear he's a ghost. I did not see him anywhere near us when we left and I've been keeping a keen eye on her."

"Alioss, he has her back. Speak to Rano. We need your strength in the camp to finish training the new arrivals."

He nodded. "Jared, do you know she does not even ask my name? Don't you find that rather odd?"

"Some are like that. It's not always the men who care less about the woman's name. Two can play at that game and I've heard she can play it very well. I've run across a few along my journeys. Then again, perhaps she already has from Rano and has no need to ask you directly."

Alioss shrugged, patting Jared on the shoulder. "I'll

see if I can get her back to the palace so I can send a courier to Rano. Unless you mention this first. I don't think it will be an issue. Although he is mighty protective of the healer."

"Consider it done. Let's see if I can have you back amongst all the other women by nightfall. They are exhausting me." Malik punched his upper arm, gathered his flock and disappeared into the thriving market. "Ladies, I leave you here. I have business to attend." With no further explanation, he strode off.

***

"Jacob, will you take these back to my chambers and leave them in the alchemy? I have someplace I will go and you will not come." Nofret grinned, not divulging any further details. "The guard will follow me on this venture, I assure you."

Nofret did not glance back as she wound through the crowded market toward her protector. She halted as a group of priests blocked her way. This was perfect timing as excitement rose up in her veins.

Maneuvering to the right and slipping down an alley, she quickly glanced over her shoulder and saw daylight. Locating the building was easy when all of a sudden the air misted over, vision blurring as a cold wind rushed and swirled around her. Then it spoke. "You must release him." But as she swung around anxiously, not a soul was there.

"But which one are you talking about?" she asked as the noise of the busy alley emerged back into her ears. Glancing up at the steps, she released a frustrated sigh and then continued up, softly rapping on the door. It swung open slightly and someone Nofret did not know spoke to her. The woman seemed to know her.

"Ah, healer, what do you do here? I do not think anyone has need of your services in these parts today."

"Correct. But allow me entrance. I need to see who

is in charge. I have a special favor to ask and it is rather urgent."

The woman glanced about quickly. "Yes. Come in. I will go and advise her now. I am sure she will see you shortly."

Nofret stood just inside the corridor, time ticking away, when finally a stately brunette approached. She was dressed in what seemed like gold particles instead of a proper day tunic. "What services do you need from us, Nofret the Healer?"

Nofret moved closer. "This is a bit delicate. May we speak in private? Is it safe enough?"

"Yes, it is."

"Okay. Well, there is something I want to do for a special man. Can I enlist your help? I know those that come from leagues away to see you perform."

She laughed. They both actually laughed. "I know there is a strong man of great worth that has his sight on you. So there is a true purpose in your arrival. I knew of it before. Now the time has come. You are here."

"Ah, why yes, of course. I should have realized you would already know."

"Come along. I will instruct you myself. Then you will have a chance to practice with some of the girls. We have a group coming in a short time. Shall we?"

"Yes. Oh, please do not call me healer. Nofret will do."

"I can do that. I am Aeroella. Now, let's get you properly attired." Together they walked into a rather large and formal dressing area housing quite a selection of garments. Glancing further, Nofret could see additional rooms.

"Oh, I should like to try on all of this. Which do you suggest?"

Glancing at the color of her eyes and skin, Aeroella handed her something that should prove to be of benefit.

Changed, Nofret swung around several times, glancing at herself in the glass. "This is just what I was hoping."

"No other has worn this. It was made by a passing gypsy woman who instructed me to hold it aside until the right moment arrived. I guess you are that moment."

"Do you know her name?"

"Unfortunately, no. She showed up on our back doorstep as I was entering and handed it to me with those instructions. Then she disappeared into the market. Never have I seen her since."

Nofret engaged her in a sly smile. She knew who it was. Glancing up at the ceiling, she felt the smile grow. "Are those other rooms yours? They look comforting and lovely."

"Yes." They continued along to a different area. Stopping, Aeroella snapped her fingers and the music began, along with the sway of her hips. "Join when you are ready."

Two hours later, sweat beading an upper lip, Nofret was moving about the room with Aeroella, very pleased with her reassertion into the fine art of erotic dancing.

"You are a natural. He will not stand a chance. For you possess skills that take some years to learn."

They laughed.

"By then women are usually a bit heavier in the hips than a man not into a drink would want. Are you ready to try the results in the big room this afternoon? No one will know you there."

"I do. But feel I may be recognized. I was under the protection of one of the guards appointed by the palace. For some strange reason, I lost him on my way here."

"Oh, I see." She grinned. "I like you, Nofret the Healer. How about we use these and cover your beautiful face. But let them see your lovely eyes?" She held out a gorgeous gauze face veil.

"Yes, this will do. How many will be out there?"

"Peer out that curtain and you will see. They come eagerly. After the performance, they normally walk off with a few of the ladies or head back to the village to their normal flock."

Nofret's jaw suddenly dropped. He was out there. Malik.

Oh, how she was going to enjoy this. When she'd overheard him proclaiming to his women he had business to attend to, he had meant this. *Typical bloke*, she thought.

"I hear the music beginning. I'd better hurry."

"I think we can take our time. Let them begin without us. I want to have the pleasure of you and I entering in together, last. Here." Aeroella handed over a small goblet of a dark, aromatic mixture.

Sipping, Nofret felt immediate results. "This is a potent mix I've tried a time or two myself. But never in the company of overeager men. How did you know it? Exactly what else are you besides the proprietor of this lovely establishment and an amazing dancer? Come now. Tell me."

"There are secrets neither of us can disclose. Right? But you are correct. I also have a list of other qualities I bring to the table. Let us forget about that for now. There is fun to be had, healer. Why not jump right off the bridge and go for it?"

They laughed.

"*Touché*, Aeroella."

"That's our drum beat. They are ready. As I heard in another time, let us go and knock them dead."

***

Nofret knew in that instance Malik did not stand a chance. She housed the element of surprise and damn if she wasn't going to use it until he begged for mercy. *Well*, she thought, giggling wantonly with the effect of the powerful elixir, or until he realized just exactly who he was really dealing with. Here and in England.

Cymbals snapping, they entered the room together and Nofret wove her way around the performers that had stopped, parting like the Red Sea, giving them a perfect lane. The twosome broke apart, dancing, displaying flesh and charm between the men sitting on plush cushions.

Circling around Malik, Nofret did not care at this point if he recognized her or not. She lifted her arms high, breasts heaving over the skimpy blue silk fabric. She watched as his eyes roamed over her entire body, heating it further. Yes, it was there. Obvious desire for them both.

Abandoning all sense of propriety, her hips swiveled right in front of his face, spinning, then slid away just out of reach of his grabbing hands. As she seduced him, arms motioning for him to come and then saying no, she glanced over his shoulder and caught sight of her bodyguard.

An extremely pissed-off bodyguard.

Shit, she thought in a haze. The attempt at ditching him had not been successful. How the hell did he know it was her in this outfit? *Fuck*, she internally screamed, *it was the earrings!*

Then she let it all go. Cares all but forgotten, she moved toward him, leaned on him, smiling and hoping he would not believe her this bold. As he grabbed her close then set her free, he whispered roughly into her veil-covered ear. "Rest assured he will find out about your antics, healer."

Laughing up into his face, she met Aeroella and they strutted away, settling into an alluring pose just as the music ended.

Quickly, she disappeared out into the corridor and hastily changed, handing Aeroella the garments. "I'm screwed." Nofret was laughing. "That damn guard found me and my cat will surely be let out of the bag."

"I can perhaps get you safely out of here if we

hurry. One quick question. Which one were you trying to torment?"

"The first. The second was the bloke I ditched when I came in here."

"I am familiar with him. Yes. You are screwed. He's as loyal as they get to the great general."

"Don't I know it. I'm sure I'll hear an earful when I see him again. But, oh what fun that was! I can't thank you enough."

"I could tell. Anytime you want to step out of your world and into ours, you just pop right on in. Now come. I will wrap these up. They are more fitting on you than anyone else inside these walls. My gift. Well, actually by way of the gypsy."

"Ah, but you danced beautifully as well. I sure hope our paths cross again. We made a great pair out there." She took the parcel tied with a leather strap, smiled, then went right out the front entrance, knowing he was there waiting.

"Alioss."

He turned abruptly, eyeing her with a devilish smile. "That was quite a performance, healer, one I should not soon forget."

"Glad you liked it. Any chance you would keep that to yourself?"

He grinned, taking the parcel from her hand. "No. He's going to find out, I'm sure. You don't have a prayer's hope in hell at this point between those that I recognized from the army, including Malik. What possessed you to do it?"

She stopped so suddenly he nearly knocked her down. "Your commander or general. Whatever it is you call him. He is what possessed me to do it."

His brows shot straight up. "If they get drunk today they may forget. But in truth, the only two that know it was you is myself and Malik. I will take care of this."

She turned, smiling, knowing this day she had won.

"Thank you. Now I have another idea. I was wondering if perhaps Jacob could take your place. I truly believe I am safe under his care and if you spend a bit of time to show him how to defend with a spear and knife, that would be of a great benefit. I do not think he would like to carry a sword."

She turned forward and broke out in laughter. For ahead of them, leaning against a wooden stall, was Jacob the Elder. "Is that right, Jacob?"

He had listened to their conversation and his eyes lit up, head nodding approval.

"He is of keen strength, I can assure you. I've had him moving heavy objects without anyone's assistance."

"You can stop now. No need to convince me. I agree. The final word will come from Rano. If he says it is okay, Jacob, someone will come and bring you to the encampment so we can begin work. I will personally train you. Now that I am familiar with her comings and goings."

Jacob produced a grin, nodding.

Malik continued on. "As I suspected, you are probably more aware than I am of these constant antics."

They had arrived back at the palace. "Thank you, Alioss." But his attention was quickly diverted, handing the parcel to Jacob. Several lovely ladies were sliding into the wading pool, naked.

She grinned, taking Jacob by the arm. "Come along. We have some mixing to do. I have half a notion you brought that all about. Making sure they did that just as we arrived. You are by far, Jacob the silent, much smarter than I."

She gave him instructions and he worked on one side of the room while she ground up seeds, started the fire pit, unwrapped the Goddess of Tawaret and placed her on a golden plate.

"By the way, I know. But I will never say a word to anyone." She smiled slyly at him as Jacob turned around, throwing his hands up in the air and then bowing in a grand gesture.

"Bring over the mixture." She had the pit blazing, throwing a handful of the sage mix on it as the air crackled with sparks, producing a quickly evaporating white smoke. He stood back, mesmerized by her magic.

"Oh, great Goddess Tawaret, I ask you to bless this statue that we honor this day with great protection over our Queen Satiah and her son to be born as next ruler. Please bring him into our world with intelligence, strength, and humanity to all peoples." She threw another handful in and the statue was engulfed.

Quickly she wrapped it for the final time and put it in the silk pouch. "I will give this to her tonight. This is all she needs. I really could leave now, for my task is done. But I doubt that I will be allowed. I am sure there is a bigger task than this in the form of Rano the Mercenary."

He smiled, shaking his head affirmatively.

"Yeah, I knew it. It's always easier to see things from the opposite side. Like yours. Anyway, will you be with me the whole time until I am finished?"

He nodded yes.

"Can you write any little bit of detailed information down? Something that I could really use? I feel like I am stubbing my toe one minute, then getting a wonderfully relaxing massage the next."

Chagrin was all over his face.

"Oh, whatever, Jacob. I am fully aware I should not have asked. But I had to give it a whirl all the same. Can't blame a girl for trying."

His eyes belied total merriment as he left her rooms and took leave.

She bathed on her own, having advised her ladies tonight they were officially free to do something else. With all this unabashed lovemaking going on all around her, it was starting to wear her thin. The less she saw the better.

At dinner she knew it would be the same. Both the Pharaoh and the queen liked the dancers and music.

That was fine, but it was what was going on all around the tables that was severely grating on her delicate nerves. More and more thoughts of Rano ran rampant through her mind. She'd not seen him in a few days. With the silk pouch in hand, she gained entry into the queen's quarters and approached slowly as her ladies in waiting were getting her ready. Bowing, she extended her hand, holding out the pouch.

"I have this for you to put on a shelf over there."

The queen took the pouch and opened it, unwrapping from the fine cloth the six-inch statue and allowing her fingers to glide over its beauty and coolness. "How did you find one so small? All the ones I've seen are of course larger than life itself."

"I had it made for me before I left my village and just finished the blessings. You do not even need to say a word to her. Just smile and place both your hands on your swelling stomach and that will be all that is required."

The queen stood, walking over to put it on the gold shelf. "Thank you, healer. I still want you to stay until I deliver. You and the wives will be here. But if you want to return to your village to help them or other villages near, I give you my blessings. A ship and crew are at your disposal."

Nofret smiled warmly, truly liking this intelligent and beautiful creature.

"I will let you know. For now, I have someone at my village who meets my qualifications and she is taking care of all their needs quite nicely. She sent me a scroll telling me things were fine. But yes. I would like to help those in the villages near here. Do you have time to post a courier out with messages that I will be free if anyone requires my services?"

"I will, but they already know of your special gifts,

Nofret. Your history came before you even arrived for the first time. That's how I heard of you myself." She smiled, taking her hands. "You do not wish to dine with us this night, I can see it."

"I am not the only one that has special gifts."

"It is not a special gift to see the yearning in the eyes of another woman and know that it's not for female companionship, but a male. He will not come this night or for several others, as he prepares for our next campaign. He has asked for the Pharaoh's permission to assign you Jacob the Elder as your guard so he can claim all his soldiers for duty. My husband has approved this request."

Nofret gazed at her questioningly. "Was that movement I just saw at your stomach? The baby moving?"

Both women smiled as the queen continued. "Have him go to the encampment at sunrise. He will stay there for a few days in preparation for his new service toward you. When Rano is satisfied, he will return. In the meanwhile, the two palace guards outside your chambers will remain there and you will promise me that you will always be with Meliah and Asofia. I know you like to go off by yourself, healer. Word has gotten back to me of certain events that took place."

She grinned and stepped back, unable to hold in a laugh. "One would think in a palace this grand and large that one could maneuver without much notice. But that is not the case. It is the truth you speak, my Queen, that I do wander off. But I give my word to abide by your full request."

"As you say by my full request, I will wonder if you will find a hole in those words that you can use to your advantage later."

Nofret raised both brows. "I will do my best to live by them. I promise."

"As it is said, so shall it be. Ladies, you are my witness of what this woman is all about."

They all started laughing.

"You are in great health, Queen Satiah, I can see it in the twinkle of your eyes. They are bright and your tone of voice is light and happy. You do not need me any longer. Of that I am completely sure. But I will stay until your son is born and then will leave. On that, you do have my word. Unless, of course, something else of major urgency takes me away."

She bowed, leaving the chambers truly feeling of light spirit herself. *Excellent,* she thought, for having Jacob the Elder. That brought out a smile. For they would indeed find some mischief to get into for sure. He'd not be able to berate her when she pulled him along on her adventures.

She went into the dining area, took a spare platter and filled it with food. Quietly, she left the room not engaging anyone in conversation. Thankfully, the room had not filled yet, as it was still early in the evening.

She nodded at the two soldiers posted outside her chambers and they promptly opened and closed her doors. Setting the food down, she walked straight out onto the balcony, immediately disobeying orders. With the ladies off tonight and Jacob the Elder doing his own thing, she was free to move about the country, so to speak. Jacob would be searched out shortly and handed that all-important scroll. Tomorrow, his day would begin entirely differently than today.

So her first course of action was the pools. It was perfect timing, as most of the palace would be joining the Pharaoh and the queen for food and entertainment. Then it struck her as she was walking through the garden area to her private section overlooking the Nile, that she'd not actually engaged him in one word. The Pharaoh. Probably never would, she thought. She'd seen him with Rano, some other guards, his servants and leaving the palace on his grandest of grand chariots. But not a syllable had passed between them.

Slipping out of the silk, allowing it to drop onto the cold marble at her feet, she slid into the crystal clear water and let her head rest back against the linen pillows. A raven squawked above her, but her eyes remained closed as she tried to disengage body from mind to see with her third eye what was to happen next.

It came to her. Not in the way of a vision, but in the way of a strong calloused hand sliding over her silky wet shoulder, cupping one breast.

Chapter Eight

She moaned as his body slid up against hers while his lips kissed the curve of her neck. A weak protest nearly formed at his lips not touching her very own. Moving her head to the side, her eyes opened.

"You!"

"Yes. Who else were you expecting?" His voice was gruff as he waded back just enough.

"I can see I will need guards to accompany me even to the water. I was believing you were fully engaged at the encampment."

"You will never need them here. I only have those keeping an eye on you when you leave since it's clear you like to roam, healer. When inside the walls, I have no need of knowing what you are about."

"So what is your business with me? State it. You know perfectly well I am naked. Did you come carousing thinking I'd just fall into your arms because you are leaving soon?" She wanted to bite her tongue for the bitterness in her tone.

He grinned, splashing water up on her shoulder and watching, mesmerized, as it slid softly down its silkiness. "What concoction do you use on that lovely skin to keep it from turning brown in this desert heat?"

She did not move. "You will not distract me. I keep my wits about me unless you prowl around when I am dozing. It will not happen again until I know you are off." She was grinning, daring him to come closer.

"But you were not safe, were you?"

"That's only because they know you are here and allowed you entry to my areas."

"Why would I not be allowed here? I am the

Pharaoh's general. I can go anyplace I choose. There is no section that is off limits to me." His knowing grin matched hers.

"Well, that may mean places, it is true. But it does not mean people, as in me. I am a favorite of the queen and you and I both know you will not just take me as you do others."

He did not budge.

But she did. Swimming close, she stood, allowing the water to swirl around her breasts. His eyes blinked twice but never left her face. Oh, she thought. He did have a will of iron.

"Your fiery tongue is anticipated and enjoyable. I will like doing battle with you verbally and between the blankets, I assure you." He rose in all his naked splendor, as her eyes and mouth dropped.

"You see? You are not indifferent to me, woman of mine. But I have known that throughout time. I wanted to come and tell you myself that Malik and Alioss are both training your Jacob the Elder. He will be back to you in three days. Should you find yourself wandering outside the palace against orders, I have those that will keep watch on you in case you decide to go where you do not belong or decide to entertain my men with your exotic dancing."

Every inch of her exposed skin turned a soft shade of pink.

"Oh. I knew someone would tell you. Who did? I was promised no word of this would reach your ears." She was grinning, unabashedly coming up the steps one at a time. Then she wove her way around him, keeping out of arm's reach while placing on her robe. It clung tightly against her wet body.

"I was there."

She stopped dead in her tracks. "You were? I did not see you."

He pulled her close, letting his hands run inside that

robe against her still dampened skin. They both felt her quiver. "I was retrieving a few items left there from a previous visit, healer, and stopped when I saw Aeroella dancing in the great room. She only does that when something is amiss. I wanted to see who she had it in for."

"Shit."

"That word I understand, Nofret, and I must say I will look forward to you dancing solely for me. I have never seen a woman move as you did. Even Aeroella was second to your swaying hips and overflowing charms."

He all but ripped the silk cloth from her body, dislodging the robe. It pooled on the marble at their feet. As he lifted her up, she wrapped her legs around his naked hips and he brought them both back into the warm waters. As he moved them toward the center of the pool, the atmosphere around them sizzled.

"I will dance for you, mercenary. Before you go to battle." She pulled his head down and kissed him wantonly. It was just not fair. He was in her blood and bones. Tonight, if he even hinted, she'd say yes.

He pulled back, releasing her and shaking his head. "There is no hope for me as a man keeping my strength with you about, love. But I would have it no other way. Will you not be more cautious when you venture out until Jacob returns?"

She shook her head no. "So you have not been told, have you?"

He left the pool, put his tunic on and fastened the gold belt before he slid into his sandals and tied them up. "What?"

"The queen this very day gave me leave to move about on my own until he does return. If I wish to go into this village or another I am free to do so."

"I think you missed something there, my lovely. There was an entire message you are leaving out in this conversation. I know it was if you would wait until Jacob the Elder returned and take him with you was what she had suggested. If I am not right."

"Damn it."

He laughed, his eyes warming tremendously as he gazed down into the pool.

Oh, how bold he was. She wanted to splash him and stomp her foot in the water, at the same time making him take her here and now. But it was futile. He waved her off and departed.

"Arrogant ass," she muttered into the darkening sky as she glanced about, noticing that the torches were already lit. When had that happened? How dare that bloke touch her like that and then depart with such indifference? She placed a finger gently on her swollen lips and smiled.

Damn! She had no choice but to take this into her own hands. Time seemed to be running out. Drying off and dressing, she pulled her knees tight against her chest and stopped, quietly listening to the locusts off in the reeds singing their nighttime song. The wind picked her hair up, moving it across her back. She had refused to wear the wigs and, seeing as they thought she was already an eccentric healer, she knew no one would demand it.

One lone fishing boat was being rowed towards its shore. She envied the fisherman's freedom. She had to know what to do next when her responsibility to the queen had been met. Was it possible that she could leave before the baby was born? Would Malik? For a long while she just sat there, not thinking of either man but listening to her inner voice prescribing a plan.

The wind blew again as she stood with a firm idea in place. As soon as Jacob returned to her they were going to set out on a mission of their own. She went back and slid into her bed, forming it fully in her mind.

When she rose the next day, she set about preparing. She did indeed not leave the palace grounds nor go to the pool without her ladies. As she gathered up supplies in the herbal room, she awaited the arrival of Jacob. At last, one day later than planned, he was allowed entry into her chambers.

She waited for the two guards to close her doors before rushing over to him. "So, was it good? Are you a full-fledged Egyptian hitman now?"

His grin produced a set of white teeth as he nodded, thrusting his mighty arms up and exposing them, to her great joy. "Excellent. Where are your weapons? In your room? Did they test you to your limits? I heard from Rano that both were training you. For their own devious purposes, I am sure. Were they like two bantering elks?"

He moved two fists towards each other and back again.

"I get it. They were. How funny that must have been. But look at you. Tanned and not looking the worse for wear. I'd say you are stronger than you want us all to believe."

He touched the side of his head.

"Yes. I agree. Smarter as well. But I'm on to you, Jacob the Elder."

He grinned, enjoying that name.

"Well, we leave at first light. I have two camels ready. I want you to go back and get your gear prepared. We are going to visit some of the villages outside Memphis and see where we can be of service. Has the army left for their campaign?"

He nodded yes and held up two fingers.

"Two days ago? What the hell. Where have you been?"

He grinned, obviously glad he did not have to reply on that one. He might look old but parts of him were still apparently quite young and arduous.

"Really? You? Without potions or magic? Oh…"

He left her then, sporting a wide, toothy grin. It was during the night when she was sound asleep and the wind blew her drapes around that she heard Rano's voice. It was as if he was leaning over her whispering into her ear.

"Valley of the Kings."

Her eyes flashed open, sitting straight up. "Oh, my God," she said into the darkness. "But we can do it. I have a ship at my disposal. Shit, yes, we can do it." She felt it. Closure was on its way of some type. She wanted to jump up and down on the cushions. Was it going to be that easy? What was she to do there? That was a burial ground. Rano was not dead yet. Why was his voice so clear in her ears when he was still alive? How could that be?

This was getting a bit too surreal.

Lying back, she tried to sleep. But a million things needed to be prepared. How was she going to get the queen to let her go that far? She could not lie; that would not be fair. Besides, before they even left port she would have heard of it from someone and prevented it. Damn. She'd have to abort her earlier plans and think about this.

Rolling over, she plotted, sighed and then gave up. It did not matter. If she was supposed to go there then the green light would go off and there would be no obstacles. Were they not headed in that direction to Lower Egypt to squash the Kush uprising that had grown momentum and now was on a big push into the territory? Had she heard Ethiopia? Shaking her head, she let it all go. It would sort itself out when it was time.

But she was so impatient. It was not like any other passage, that was clear. Nor was she the same person who had left Venice on that fine day and found herself in Victorian England.

The next day when Jacob the Elder arrived with a scroll in hand, she was eating outside. His face said it all. He was anxious. Glancing at him while unrolling the parchment, she read the bold and now familiar script of their queen.

"You must leave at once. My sage had a vision that

someone of great importance may need your healing at the impending battle in the southern lands. Go quickly. Take your man and what you need, but hurry. Time is of the utmost. The ship is readied and awaits your arrival."

"Crap. This is both good and bad news. She does not mention who the vision was about. Surely it can't be the king, or even in her pregnancy she'd travel to be closer." Nofret rose, sending the goblet off the table. Jacob leaned down and replaced it. "I know. My nerves are rattled. This is exactly how I felt when I arrived in another time and did not know how I got there or how to get back home. I was lost."

He patted her on the back.

"Okay, enough self-indulgence, right? Are you ready?" He nodded, pointing to a large carpet bag, weapons protruding out. "Wow, do you have ESP? Do you know what that is?" He ignored her just then as he quickly went about gathering up jars, herbs, salves and jugs.

"Okay, you keep doing that and I'll grab better clothes for the desert. I can't go scampering about on board that ship and probably a mule or camel looking like Queen Sheba of Arabia," she mumbled to no one, for as she turned to look at him, he had vanished. "Well, what the hell."

He reappeared from another chamber, motioning rapidly at the scroll and moving his finger quickly.

"Of course, I will write a reply." Dipping the reed in ink, she hastily scribbled a note back to the queen advising they were preparing to depart on the awaiting ship shortly. "Just hand this outside the door to the guard and we will leave out through my balcony. It's a quicker route down to the docked ship."

She hoisted one bag onto her arm and the smaller one as well. Jacob took three and they walked rapidly down to the awaiting crew. Indeed, they were prepared to shove right off. The second her sandals hit the deck, the plank was pulled away.

She was shown below where she could store her items and spend the night. She stayed there, not bothering to unpack or go up. She had changed hastily back at the palace and more than a few male eyes had squinted at her adjusted female attire. But she cared not.

So what she had a male tunic on over her wrap? It was a hell of a lot more practical. Especially if she had to run or rip the damn thing off and still have freedom to move. This was not modern day Saudi. It was ancient Egypt. She could actually get away with this. Particularly under the blessings and protection of Queen Satiah.

A rap at the door got her attention and she opened it to a tall man with a small tray of food and drink. She took it, kicking the door closed with her foot and feeling some semblance of courage since Jacob was on board. Until she needed him again, or he decided to have one of his strange conversations, she'd leave him to his own devices as he would her.

Restless and eating little, she drank even less, as her stomach was in upheaval. Not by the pitching of the ship, but by a clear internal message that someone was in trouble and someone else was going to die. Who was it?

She could hear men's voices in her head and stopped to wonder if she'd just imagined something going on between Rano and Malik? Or was it just the voices from above or below where the oarsmen were being urged on by the helmsman to row harder until the wind hit the sails?

She had no clue.

Opening the door in frustration, she moved up to the deck and stood the night away with the working men until sunrise. Finally, she strode over to the closest one.

"How far down the Nile have we come?"

"Between Beni Suet and El Minya."

She nodded, moving back when she saw Jacob heading her way. Damn, even silent, she was happy to have his presence. He looked none the worse for wear, so obviously, he had received a good night's sleep. She nodded him closer. "We are nearer now to El Minya. The battle I overheard was to be near the Valley of the Kings in Edfu. That means we are on the river another twenty-four hours. I heard them say a strong northern wind was starting to blow and would move us faster. This is good, look, the oars are raised and sails full."

He made a small pyramid with his thumbs and pointer fingers.

"Exactly. That's what I think too. We will get off in Luxor if the battle is in Edfu. Then we can set up a camp of some type. I still am not sure why I'm needed specifically. But we are both headed in the right direction."

She grasped for a quick breath. "Will I ever hear your voice, Jacob the Elder?"

He nodded yes.

"Good. I want to know what you sound like."

She was done talking. Standing there at the railing, she only left it to relieve herself in the pot below and eat. She did not sleep. He did not sleep. Together they stayed side by side, watching the shore get closer and move away as the Nile weaved like a snake through the land.

She watched the captain's approach.

"Healer, here are your items. We are landing shortly. The ship will stay as most will go ashore to ensure your safe passage to Luxor. There you are to set up camp."

"Do you know for how long?"

"No, you will await orders."

"Thank you. We are ready."

Chapter Nine

The drums could be heard, their steady rhythm growing louder and stronger as they approached the enormous encampment. Her eyes bulged out. All she could see in every direction was thousands of soldiers and tents. *Oh, my God*, she thought. This was just what a blockbuster movie set would look like in the future. Mini camps inside the larger-scale one were formed for provisions, horses, and camels. As well as continued training and sleeping quarters.

As it grew larger and larger, Nofret and Jared were met by a familiar face covered with desert dust and a warrior's helmet. She knew him well enough.

"Healer, Jared the Elder."

Nofret spoke for them both. "Alioss, hello. I don't know if it is good to see you or not. Where are we to go?"

He turned his horse around. "To where the other women healers are. They have already established their supplies and are readying for our battle."

There was no reply. She did not have one in her right now, realizing that of course there would be injuries and death.

"Rano himself will not come. Explicit instructions will be handed down and brought to you. Set up your own tent as you see fit. It has been raised over there with the flying colors of the House of Rano. This will keep you both safe from any internal camp strife. I wish I could say the same to you, healer, that it is good to see you. But perhaps more men stand a chance of survival with your skills."

She was indeed touched by his proclamation as he turned and pulled the horse's reins, leaving them in a cloud of dust.

She turned toward Jacob. "So you are to stay with

me. Good, I am glad to have heard that. I have never seen anything of the likes of this. Jacob, have you?"

He shook his head yes.

"Oh my, poor you." Then she halted their progress. "Was it because of me?"

Again he shook his head yes.

"Come on." The camels lowered, kneeling on the dirt. "Let's get in there and see what we are dealing with. At least here we are actually doing something of use. Look way over there in the distance. I can see the tallest of the pyramids. Even from here they are indeed an amazing sight."

As the camels brought them the short distance into the encampment, they remained quiet until their feet were back on the sand and they walked side by side with their bags.

"I overhead a couple of the women assigned to me back at the palace gossiping. Anyway, they were talking about the Pharaoh. I was not really paying it much attention at the time, but then it dawned on me. Now I understand what I heard. I guess he has several wives. But Satiah is his first one. If she bears a son she will potentially rule should he pass on. Until the boy is of age. Now it truly becomes imperative she bears a healthy one that rises to power. Or she will be moved down in the wife rankings. Imagine that."

He touched her arm, possibly hoping to alleviate all that pent-up nervousness.

She smiled at him. "I know, I am rambling. Once I get busy, I will shut up."

That toothy grin appeared.

She went inside the tent and was surprised at how roomy it was in comparison to what it looked like on the outside. "We'd better set up what we can. Can you move that damn scorpion out of here? I have no patience for those ungodly creatures. Anyone who's crazy enough to worship them is positively nuts. Surely he will just get in the way and I'll have to kill him."

Gently, Jacob prodded him along, using a long-handled reed sweeper.

"That's better. Now take a look around and see if we can keep those dang things out. I can deal with many creatures, but the thought of those moving about while I sleep is disturbing enough."

He roamed about, nodding that the coast was clear. She finished unpacking their supplies, laying them out for quick access. "We'd better prepare some ointments for wounds, rip up some of that linen for bandages and mix up some powders in case they need a swifter means of leaving this earth."

Three hours later they had established an advance on what they would surely need when the battle started. "I'm going back out there and see who wants to talk and find out what they know. I smell food being cooked. I don't know if we have to get it ourselves, or someone has been appointed. This does, though, seem to be a well-oiled machine."

Nofret approached several women dressed in multi-fabric tunics, which dictated the village they hailed from. They were not Egyptian.

***

"Healer Nofret, a welcome to you and Jacob the Elder. We watched your arrival and were notified you would be joining our group. I am here to advise that you are in charge of our quarter. When you are fed and have had water, come with me. My name is Neira. Unfortunately, we do not have the luxury of much time for me to tell you who everyone else is. I'll leave that up to you to discover if you feel the need."

Nofret nodded. "There are many. How many healers do we have gathered in total?"

"Sixteen, including you. The rest are from other

villages who were brought along due to the massive size of the king's army alone. Someone thought ahead and gathered more to help."

Nofret glanced around at the large gathering, noticing the frightened look on most of their desert-weathered faces.

"Are they here with full knowledge of what may not only happen out there, but to them as well?"

Neira's reply was a bit to clipped for Nofret. "Does that matter? They will do as asked. They have not been given any other choice."

"Ah, I see. It's just easier if someone wants to help instead of being held in bondage. But I do understand."

Neira eyed her skeptically as Nofret withstood the appraisal. "You are not Egyptian? I was under the impression that you are since you came from the palace."

"What, because I dress differently? Well, let me assure you that I am. Also here under full blessings of our queen. Anything else you want to know? I am not opposed to you asking now while there is still time. After that, it will be too rushed for such small talk." Her own wall was up and it would stay there. This woman did not need to know any more than was told to her in the way of instructions.

But Neira was ballsy and persisted. "And the man?"

"He is Jacob the Elder. He is my assistant and extremely capable of taking care of anything asked of him including drawing a sword if necessary. He may look like an elder, but he is quick of wit and strength. He does not speak. But let me assure you he does comprehend with utmost intelligence everything that is going on around him."

"Ah. I understand. So I recommend you keep him with you."

This woman was starting to piss Nofret off. So she pushed back. "Just so I am clear, where do you come from and what is your role in all of this? Are you a healer?"

"I am Hebrew. My village was destroyed, my girls sold off and my sons bore into labor over there building the final pyramid." Her voice was tinged with sarcasm.

Her plight did not touch Nofret's heart. Something about her warranted closer examination. "Your husband, where is he?"

"Bondage like my sons. I was told I could work in the village. There were no other choices offered to me. I am merely a slave under the king."

"How are you a healer? What do you know?"

"My grandmother and my mother were both gifted with special healing touches and a mind to know how to help others discovering what ailed them. I also have this. Why don't you come with me to my tent? I will show you what has been prepared."

Following along, Nofret could not resist the urge and stuck her tongue partially out at Jacob. He shook his head back and forth, trying to hold back a laugh at her bold sassiness.

Nofret surveyed the scene inside Neira's tent. "I see potions and dried goods mixed properly. Your oils and tonics are the correct color, mix, and quantity. You are indeed good at what you know, Neira. When you decide to say my name it would be easier to use Nofret and not 'healer,' as I think others here would look to answer you as well."

"But you are above us all and we know that."

Their gaze steadied. Neither one was willing to give a fraction of an inch.

Nofret needed to straighten this out right now. "I am not of higher value than anyone else here. Man or woman. In my eyes we are equals."

Neira released her gaze as Nofret continued. "You seem to know what's going on all around us. So, when are they marching to battle and where is it to take place?"

Neira hesitated a second and then answered. "The

Kush army is already encamped in Kom Ombo. They will meet the army somewhere in between Luxor and there. The Egyptian army stretches from here to near the border of Edfu."

Nofret was a bit taken aback by the details. "That's incredible. I would think it uncommon for a healer to know who is where and when they will battle. Especially knowing how your people can be treated."

Neira bristled at the reference to how she would come to know such things as Nofret watched her closely. "I was taking care of a man that had been injured during training and was brought to me. He eventually took fever and rambled on like I was his companion on the battlefield. I do not think he realized what he was saying."

"Oh, so it was just talk? The ramblings of a sick man?"

Neira seemed to be very careful. "It could be. Why don't you ask the commander? You are under his protection, are you not?"

"What gave you that notion?"

"The stripes on your tent. They are the same that are found in high ranking people that show allegiance to the king and queen."

"Now, how would you know such things? More rumors?"

"I apologize, healer. I got carried away. Having been out in encampments before, I was quickly educated on where I could and could not go and was warned to never go into the area where the larger tent with yellow markings was."

"No apology needed. But you are correct to acknowledge that those words may get you into trouble someday. I will not, though, be a part of that process. Just be careful is all I can say to you now."

"I know," Neira stuttered. "We should go out; the food will be ready." She held her tent flap open as Nofret passed outside, noting where it sat in the midst of this part of the encampment.

Eyeing the much-talked-about striping, a slight grin formed. She still did not know precisely when they would do battle. Well, perhaps those in this section were not allowed to go further into the encampment. But Nofret sure as hell would if it became necessary.

"Healer, I am four tents down from yours."

That brought another smile to her face as she stopped and was handed a plate of cooked meat. "You did mean to say Nofret, right?"

Neira eyed her with a grin, locking horns with those dark brown orbs once again. "Yes, exactly."

They sat down opposite as she joined Jacob. "You lucky man. I will not hear a complaint coming from you ever. Especially now that you are surrounded by all these women. I hope you have been making yourself useful."

He bit off a piece of the meat and drank of the water, watching her closely. It was still ninety degrees even at this time of the afternoon with the sun beating down on them in full force.

She glanced over to the viewable tip of one of the pyramids off in the distance and was sucked into a moment where she saw a procession of heavily decorated soldiers carrying a box encased with...

Jacob nudged her, holding out the liquid.

"Damn, I had something going on there before you interrupted me. But thanks. I am parched." She drank deeply of the coldness, quenching her thirst. Then she rose, washing her plate and stacking it back with the others. "I'm going for a walk. Make yourself useful and come along with me."

He held up his hand and shook his head.

"Why? Can you sign me on this one?"

He pointed to the ground.

"You want us to stay right here?"

He nodded yes.

"I can't sit still. I'm filled with anxiety right now, Jacob. I have to move. What do you suggest I do, walk in circles?"

Again he nodded yes.

"Damn it," she whispered close to his face. "Okay, fine."

She had pressed down a good inch of desert sand, forming a large oval behind her tent. Then she looked up and saw Alioss coming toward her with a horse in tow. He leaped off, leaving the ropes dangling. Walking over, he picked her up and set her up on the other, handed her the reins, and climbed back on his.

"He wants to see you." They trotted through the enormous encampment as it spread out in every direction imaginable to the naked eye. It took nearly thirty minutes by horseback before she reached what she knew was the center of the army. Sliding off the mare and walking behind him, she noticed the colors of his tent matched her own.

Her heartbeat increased.

He was indeed a smart man. Being in the center of several tents all flying those exact same colors would outsmart any that were bold enough to infiltrate and think they could sweep in during the darkest hours of the night and kill him.

She locked eyes with Alioss, noticing he seemed restless.

"What are you waiting for? Go in. Don't keep the general waiting. I will be right outside ready to take you back."

She moved hesitantly through the flap and halted just inside. He was pacing about, similar to what she had been doing making her steady circle in the sand just a while ago. She glanced over to the makeshift bed made of woven blankets. In one corner were his battle armor and that glorious sword that she was extremely fascinated by.

"Woman, you can touch it. I'm quite sure, though, that it is too heavy for you to lift. You may have a recollection of seeing it before."

"I know."

He turned his body right behind hers. "You do, don't you?"

"Some of it, yes. Some of it, no. I am still trying to figure out what the bloody hell I've done wrong so I can right it. Only you and one other would understand that I am not a raging lunatic right now."

She slid her hand over the coolness of the heavy blade, knowing the death that it would bring. "This you made. I know that. But where did you get the jewels? They are exceptional."

"I believe someday you will have them if I am not mistaken."

She shook. Did he understand? She would indeed someday have them. But why? Did he take them off before battle and give them to her? Was that why she was here now?

Something was truly screwed up.

"You once said some women will not share their thoughts when they look as far away as you do right now."

She moved closer, only a few inches separating them from the much-wanted contact. "Yes, I did say those exact words."

He moved so only the thickness of a thin thread separated them.

"This time I will share them with you. But rather than with words of which I can produce too many, I will use my touch."

His eyes turned dark as he stood still.

"Mercenary, I did not bring my costume to dance for you. There was no time. If you want me to not do this, you must tell me to stop right now."

He did not move. Nor speak.

She untied her belted robe, letting it drop, followed by her heavier tunic and lighter wrap. Before him, she stood naked.

His muscles tightened as she moved forward, untying his gold threaded leather belt and letting it drop to his sandaled feet. His breath was deep on her face as she removed the clasps holding his custom tunic and it slid down into a heap.

All they both had on now were sandals.

She moved into his arms, strong arms that encircled her slim waist. Slowly, she slid palms down his rippled chest, memorizing again the firmness. His skin was warm. Her heart was pounding rapidly inside her bosom.

Eyes locked, he held her spellbound. Without knowledge, one hand glided down, resting gently against his raised manhood. He moaned but remained still.

Oh, she thought. *What control he has!*

"You brought me to this, mercenary."

"We should have had more time at the palace, Nofret. I had not requested you here for this in truth, my love. I wanted but your company. To make sure you are settled."

She tilted her head back as one of his hands wove through her silky hair, down her back and over the curve of her buttocks. She felt their roughness wanting more. But then stopped when she felt something familiar against her skin.

"You have it?"

He smiled into her eyes. "Yes, when the wind would have claimed it, I decided it would be mine."

"Oh, Rano." She let those lips take hers as she moved one of his hands between her dampening thighs.

His finger went inside. "Woman, you have no idea how I have wanted our reunion."

"Oh, there you are wrong. Yes, I do. Your voice has been calling me back for a very long time." She moaned, arching as his strong grip kept her upright when her knees threatened to buckle. "I wish I could have danced for you."

He chuckled, taking her with him to the rough blankets. "I will not die this day, my sweet. You could dance for me right now. But in an entirely different way than the one you shared with that room full of men."

She turned, kneeling in front of him. Her heart was already shattering and there was no way to stop it. This was when she became completely aware of what she was doing and thinking.

At last.

Gently she touched his heated skin to discover how ready he really was. A strong gush of wind suddenly threw apart the heavy canvas tent flaps, swirling around them both. Then it evaporated back out the way it had come, closing them shut.

He pillaged her lips as all thought in both shut down. Her nails dug deep into his strong muscles as he lifted her up and took what was rightfully his. All of her. She moaned as he sat up, holding her tight, forcing a union so powerfully potent she started to cry, having never been filled with such love before.

They both shook, releasing, as he kissed each tear while it fell streaming down her cheeks. No man who called for death should ever have such a gentle side, she finally thought, as her breathing slowly turned to normal.

"I think I may have left my own special brand of marking on you, mercenary." She looked him square in the eyes. "I love you."

"Yes, you do. It took you long enough."

She tried to jab at his ribs but he caught her hands, shoving her down on the rough blankets, hovering above as she felt him grow inside again. When he released her wrists, she grabbed his neck, tugging his head down to hers and kissing him deeply.

He pulled back. There was something very

important that needed to be said. "Woman, you know I am in love with you. A hundred years before I was even alive, I knew I loved you."

Her voice was raspy, barely above a whisper, struggling to get something out as he watched her intently, waiting.

She finally managed, "Thank you for not giving up on me." Her hand was over his heart as one last tear fell.

Leaning down, he scooped her tightly into his arms.

Her unspoken words nearly mirrored his. Soon, she would have to let him go for good. But this was not the mood either wanted in his tent right now.

"I think I'll tuck these clothes of yours away and keep them. Forcing you to ride through camp on bareback. That should fire up all my men."

"Smart ass."

"Ah, my sweet. You are my life. I should have just taken you back at the palace and forced you to be my wife."

"Never mind that. Ask me now, here. We do not need the blessings of the Pharaoh to know we belong to each other."

"I will do no such thing. Yes, we do need his approval and you know that. Otherwise, you are no more than my mistress, since we do not share common quarters back at the palace. Perhaps you would not mind that at all?"

There it was. That damn roguish grin reappearing.

"Fine. I was never one to like things nailed down in writing anyway. Must be some kind of commitment issue I have."

They both laughed. "You sure do."

She scoffed, feigning indifference without much success. "Anyway, you have something of me. What shall I have of you?"

Oh no, she suddenly thought. *Is this when he will remove the jewels from his sword and give them to me?*

Thankfully, he did not budge.

"Women. Always wanting more. Did you not just rake my body with yours? Do you need to have me again?"

She laughed up into devilish dark eyes. "Yes. I want more. A lot more. But we are out of time right now, great mercenary."

He reached for her but was met with thin air. She was now out of his arms and searching for all her belongings, laughing. "If I can find everything I came with, I will dress and go back to my people. If I stayed any longer, they will all know what went on here and who summoned me to do it. Although I care little for idle gossip, I do care if it involves me."

He stood, taking her roughly against his nakedness. "Fine, go. But come back before we go to battle. I will send someone else next time. Be prepared. I won't keep either one of us waiting long."

***

She tied the belt around the final layer, turning as he lifted one side of the tent flap. "I will come whenever you ask it of me."

He partially blocked her exit. "Wait, one more thing."

"Yes?"

"Did the queen truly believe it is the king that's in danger?"

Her eyes locked with his while she blatantly lied. "I do not know. But I'm here in case anything like that happens."

She dropped the flap, quickly locating Alioss chewing on a reed. Her demeanor altered slightly as along beside him was Malik. She refused to look at both but addressed Alioss while staring off in the distance.

"Are you coming?" Even to her own ears her voice sounded agitated.

Alioss shook his head. "Malik will bring you back. I

just received special parcels that are in need of urgent review with the General."

"Which is it truly, Alioss? Commander or general? Anyway, never mind. But he said it would be you that does it."

His gaze roamed over her swiftly, apparently wondering why she felt bold enough to question his judgment in this trifle situation. "Go, healer." Alioss stood back, letting Malik take control.

Who put his hands on those all-familiar hips and slid her up onto the horse as she took the ropes. As they moved back at a slower pace, she looked down at her own white knuckles and tried to get her brain engaged.

"It's all right," was all he said as they wove through the encampment. "It has to be. If it is any consolation, I was told only that which we really needed to recall would remain in our memory after we move on.

"It will all become very clear to us both when it is necessary, Healer Nofret. Until then, I ask you to bury all those worries away. They are not needed here right now. Neither of us have been angels and were not asked to come here to do so. But, before we close this subject for good, I'd like to ask you one question."

"Go ahead."

"Do you recall all the details of being here before?"

"No. Not all of it. Truth is, I do not know what is in store for me this time. I have just a brief recollection of knowing you here. In the future, well, that is a different story. I know we have a strong connection. Here, it is Rano. I am truly sorry if that hurts you."

He smiled. A very genuine one. "I am not sure I was here when you and Rano originally met. I am convinced this time I came to make sure something happens differently. What that is I am still not clear about."

"Again, more damn gibberish. I am fully aware you can't just tell me what's important to know and be done with it. I get it."

All of a sudden something violently flashed before her eyes.

***

He was caught off guard at what he was witnessing. Again.

"Oh my God, Malik, how many times have we done this?"

He was so relieved she had asked. "Enough. We have both been allowed to remember certain things so that we can change what was and fix this for good."

That got her attention.

He grinned. "Well, if we can recall any of this when the timing is right, we can compare notes. Now enough. Here you are, Healer Nofret. Back within the safe confines of your site."

***

She slid off the horse, tossing him the ropes. He tossed them back. "You may want to keep her handy in case you want to jaunt off later. I think you know the way by now and certainly, do not need a chaperone." He tugged on the ropes, moving his own horse around, and then disappeared.

As she tied it up, a stranger, somewhat resembling Mrs. Baker, brought water and feed. She was too beat to stop and evaluate her more closely. What the hell? Everyone seemed to either look familiar or were trying to push her in this or that direction. Enough. She was tired.

Slipping into her tent, she did not bother disrobing. Tugging the blankets up, she closed her eyes and drifted off into another troubling sleep.

As the next day passed, she knew he would not come to her. That would cause too much of a commotion. After putting in a full day of preparations and meeting others inside their special area of the camp, she finished cleaning the dinner plates.

"Jacob, I am going into the encampment. I will be

back later on." She ignored his knowing smile while untying the rope attached to the brush. Grabbing the horse's mane, she swung up and took the most central path deep into the camp. When she arrived at Rano's tent, he was just walking back from where most of his lieutenants were encamped.

A wide grin lifted light up into his handsome features. It was clear. He truly was glad to see her. She slid down off the horse as he took the rope and tied it to a branch. Opening up the tent flap, she turned toward him just as it fell in place, giving them some much-needed privacy.

"Wipe that satisfied look on your face. In here, or wherever we do this, we are equals. May I repeat what I said to you earlier since you forgot those words so quickly? You do not own me."

"Yes, I do."

"No, you do not."

He reached behind his tunic and removed a scroll from his belt. "For you, woman."

She read the document. One hand clutched it tightly while she lifted on tiptoes, kissing him as strong arms encircled her petite waist.

"Husband?"

"Signed by the king himself."

"You really must think pretty highly of me then."

Clothing now off, he slapped her naked bottom. "And I shall properly claim my bride now." He gallantly brought her into his arms as if he was crossing a fictitious threshold. The special one reserved for newlyweds. Then he set them both down onto the rough blankets.

Now he would know her just as well as she knew him. As he moved his tongue and lips down her neck, pausing only briefly at her luscious breasts, she seized an abundant amount of the blanket, hanging on for dear life as her back automatically arched.

Oh yes. He had found her out. She was indeed his.

But he was not done.

He lifted her legs up over his shoulders and plundered her with such might her back felt sensitive from the roughness of the blanket. Neither cared.

Upon mutual release, he lowered, encompassing her body, mind, heart and soul with his entire being. She gazed in wonder as the muscles in his arms contracted. Their eyes locked as a silent message carrying the weight of more than passion passed between them.

His voice was deep as he spoke first. "I had a vision of you long ago."

"You did? Why did it take so long for you to come?"

"I do not know. I am trying to figure that out. As we prepare for battle, I also had another vision that you would be here to heal me."

"That's the queen's vision. She told me in a scroll that she saw danger for someone. It must not have been Thutmose III, but you."

"Or both."

"No, it must be you."

He kissed her, again running one hand through silky, long hair. "You are not a conformist. You do not wear a wig nor parade around with glitter on your eyes. I was drawn to you even in my dreams. Our time here will not be long. But it is a love that spans many centuries. When it is time for me to leave you, Nofret, for good, I want you to remember these moments and then let me move on."

Oh, how she loved him. No wonder she was here. It was to give him final peace at last. To ensure the correct future for her and a whole lot of other people. To stop being selfish, arrogant and willful.

His eyes pierced beyond her heart to her soul. It was as if, she thought, he could read her mind and knew the struggles she had been going through.

"You are right. I do not own you. Equals we have been and shall always be. I just do not have any will left to be kept your prisoner any longer."

She released a sigh inside their tent. Hope rose. He gathered her up into his arms and they made love one more time.

Chapter Ten

"You will take leave of me now, woman. Very soon I will have a tent full of men and I won't have any snide retorts against you. Not as if any of them would dare, but you never know with this crew. At least they should not be so lusty, having been entertained very well before your arrival."

"So you say this was not planned? That you knew I was coming here all along?" As Nofret dressed he attempted to pull her backward against his bare skin.

"You must, as you say, let me go now. I will not have them seeing me like this." He laughed loudly as she jumped up and completed dressing in quick order. "You had better get a move on. I hear them coming." He reached over and swatted her ass.

"Shit. You are right." They both laughed as she slid to her knees and crawled out the back, letting the tent drop into place just as they walked in. His grin was engaging as the men eyed each other, glancing about the otherwise empty area.

"Commander?" One stepped forward, "Unless you have her hidden, what the hell has gotten into you?"

He turned, filling a goblet and motioning them all over to partake. Not a sign of her was left except the rumpled blankets and no one would give a care about that. "Did you bring the maps, Malik?"

"Yes." He rolled them out, indicating the area around them and the latest movement of the Kush tribes. "They are on the move. I just rode back into camp and have left behind two spotters and a relay so we can have updated details this evening. I highly suggest that we prepare to move out and begin our preparations across the encampment. You advise and I'll dispatch a courier with details to the healer's area."

"How much time do we have?" He rolled up the maps, putting them back in the camel leather pouches. "Three days, if we want to ride out night after tomorrow. The perfect location has been assigned. It is on the lower grounds of the desert."

"Excellent. Continue training those that need it. Make sure it is properly coordinated with supplies to the men. How many did you calculate?"

"Approximately ten thousand, commander. I did not view any superior weapons. But I am sure they would not be so reckless and expose those. Behind their encampment there were caves. I have men going in tonight to investigate and report back by tomorrow."

Rano patted Malik on the back, nodding for the other men to leave. "Go ahead and send that dispatch to the women. Did you eat and drink yet?"

"No, I reported right in. I'm headed to bathe before I visit anyone. I can't have them turn noses up at my stench." Malik grinned. "You know where I'll be if you need me." He turned, the last to exit.

"Wait." Ranof halted him. "I want to run something by you."

***

That surprised Malik. He sure as hell hoped it was not about the healer. He was not in the mood to hear about her right now. He had reined in his emotions. Locked them up and was not going to release them for any reason. Now or later.

Besides, he had found solace in the arms of a very pretty village woman who had lost her husband last year and was in no way going to make demands on him or produce any offspring when he finally left here. It was common knowledge she was barren.

Rano handed him the goblet full of red wine. "The

truths will be told this night. Sit. It is not a command, but a request. For you see, Jared Malik, Chieftan of the Semites, I am fully aware of who you are. Now I mean you to know who exactly I am."

The two stared, neither giving in. Some major conclusion was drawn as Jared relented and sat down on one of the rough blankets. "How in the hell did you find that out? It has been a well-guarded secret."

"Simple. I was the one that left you for dead. I knew you'd be found and cured by the healer."

"How did you know that? Her? I thought you had not met yet." He paused, shaking his head back and forth, listening to a soft voice clearing up a few things inside his brain. "I see. You had met her before. She arrived long before I did."

"Yes. She and I began again our relationship prior. You were delayed in coming for a purpose. An important purpose. Now I will fill you in."

Apprehension filled Jared's gut. It was the same feeling he'd had in those fleeting moments back at the museum before he found himself down in the sand. His brows drew in. Frustration mounted, followed by acute anger. Was he being played for a fool now?

"I will not mince words with you just days before a major battle. What are you specifically referring to?"

Placing his hands on broad hips, Rano stepped closer, taking a moment to listen to sounds outside the tent. When satisfied, he continued. "We are brothers, Jared Malik. At birth. Born as twins. Our mother feared for your life. You were not as strong as I and her body tired after producing many daughters. Much to the disappointment of our father. She was worried. Or so I have been advised since my recollection of her is so vague.

"Choices had to be made and she did it after hard deliberation. Our father was never to know that two of us were born. One being sicklier than the other. She sent you away to a healer woman and her husband in the Semite village nearby. You were raised as their very own. They already had five healthy boys. So you blended right in. Eventually strengthening and thriving."

Jared ran a hand up through dark, thick hair. "More and more questions I've had are now being answered. This is making sense. You were meant to be with her here. I later. But how did you find out? How long have you known?"

"I just recently found out."

"When? How did you know it was me out on the battlefield? Why did you not reach out to me during all those years like you did her?"

"I did. I don't think you were paying me much attention. Nofret was your main focus. Regardless, it was the old woman that raised you who found me prior to that last battle. She was brought to me in a frenzy and told me about your past. She was not a lunatic at all, although close to hysterics. She described you down to your weapon, clothing, horse, and, most important, the indent under your skull. I had to pay attention. The gods were willing it. If she had not done so, I would have just killed you and left you for your people to bury. It appears we were both robbed by our mother of a brother."

He felt under his back neck. It was unique.

"There is no way you would have seen that under my hair."

He laughed. "True. I hold no magical powers like our healer does. I cannot see through anyone. It was the stripe on your garment. She sewed it on when she gave it to you. The care you needed to survive would come from Nofret. Especially that you would live and we would meet. Although I was not aware of the circumstances that would bring us together. Just that it would happen. Here you are."

"Was she an old woman living high up in one of the caves outside my old village?"

"No, I was told by one of the queen's."

"Did she see my Semite stripe? Did she know I was coming without knowing why?"

"No. It had been removed and replaced with plain clothing. She did not know what you were. How you were raised. Only that my brother from afar was going to join me here. When I was told that, I set up a few men outside the village to make sure when you left I had the right man. Once I laid eyes on you myself, I knew it to be so."

He extended his hand.

Jared glanced at it long and hard, and then reached and clasped it strongly. "Brother."

"Yes. You will fight alongside me in battle. But there is something more. Of utmost importance. Much more so than what we will see out there. As I know it, I will not live much beyond that. Even the gentle, loving hands of Nofret will not be able to save me."

"What are you talking about?"

"I've made the same mistake over and over again by loving her and not letting her go when I die. Did you not know you've been here before? Several times? She as well? We are almost a love triangle except I marry her. I know your memory has been tampered with and why. Yet I am fully aware of your buried feelings. The eyes see it and do not lie, brother."

"You married her? When?"

"Ah, there it is. Pain. Don't hang on to it. For it will be short-lived, as will I."

"You seem to know so much more. I have started to have visions of things I've not seen before since I've been here. I know I have to finish something, but it's not clear to me what that is. Yet I definitely have a hand in it."

"Yes. When I die do not let her mourn. Because she will. Again and again. It is important that she not be allowed to remove even one of the jewels off my sword. Although she will think about it and try. Removing them all and storing them in a special pouch. That healer of ours is a fighter to the last breath. Hers, yours or mine. You have given in all these times. Hell, so have I. But now neither of us can. I am tired. I am ready to let her go so she can know peace and a future with you. I've seen it."

Jared stood rooted to the spot, mesmerized, as a blast of cold wind carried thousands of voices around him. Voices he knew. Alwen, Mrs. Hoyt, Father G, Victor and a whole legion of others. Swirling before his eyes, it finally subsided as a true strength rose up from inside. Yes, Malik was determined as never before.

They stood, clasping hands again. "Rano, I will make sure. I vow. Now, I must go and bathe. I will return shortly and we can eat and discuss our plan. As forewarned and forearmed as I can be against her, the better it will be for us all. I shall not think about the love you share and pray that in the future I soon let it go and forget it all."

"So be it, Jared. Now go. This time we do this together."

"Will she return back to you soon?"

"Yes. At dark. When the camp settles for the night. This time, my brother, we are going to do this right."

Jared went to his tent, brought out a fresh tunic and went to the pool and bathed. Swimming in the cool water felt refreshing after eating for two days the dust of the desert. As he looked up at the galaxy, brilliantly displayed above, it all came back as the floodgates opened wide. He rose, dressed and on his way by his tent, threw in the dirty garments and headed back to his brother's. Not even pausing to announce himself, he strode right in.

The food and drink were prepared. He sat down and ate with a hearty appetite. "Tastes a damn sight better than what I took with me." The wine dribbled down his right side and he wiped it away with the back of one hand. "Damn nuisance of a woman, isn't she? Haunts you, haunts me."

Rano sat down, laughing. "You got that right. It's high time she let go of me so I can roam the heavens. I hear there are some mighty fine wenches up there."

"The results are going to be different this time. Damn, but something has been plaguing me. Why has it taken so long for us to get this right?"

"Her. She does not like to let go of that which she loves. Do you not know that even back in England?"

"Oh, my fucking word. Can you see the future? Strange how hard it has been for me to see the past. Anyway, it's the opposite there. I'm the one that has been chasing her around. I assure you. Since the moment I saw her in Italy. She's different there than here."

"Nope, you are wrong. She's got control of you there like she has control of me here. She is a powerful healer and a sorceress rolled into one gorgeous woman. She uses all her lovely vices to keep us both under wrap."

Jared thought about that. Times and places were layering one over the other as he recalled how she'd acted so indifferent to him when she first moved into his estate. How she used certain moments out of the public eye to make sure he partook of her womanly pleasures. But then she'd meandered off, not wanting a commitment.

He grinned. "There is a man's sturdiness inside of there, isn't it?"

Rano matched his grin with a laugh. "Nope, her strength surpasses even toughened warriors such as us. Using her brain like a man and her body like a woman. Deadly combination. But we've got her all figured out this time. It's only taken three repeats."

"So what will happen if we are successful?"

"You are going to have a merry chase on your hands in earnest. As she will be pissed to high hell over the fact that I'm no longer accessible."

"But I still will be, won't I? I'm not quite finished with her yet."

"All yours, brother. You may find yourself spending the next century trying to lure her back to you like I've been. But for entirely different reasons."

"Well now, maybe then it's time we just go our separate ways so I won't be tortured for as long as you have been?"

"You have to decide what's better. I can't answer that. So, just in case she does an about face on us both, I've got a plan. Now listen, I was talking with the sage before we marched out and here is what she told me specifically we must do together and what you will do after that to make sure this is the last time."

***

Their two voices could hardly be heard, muffled as they were, just outside of the tent to anyone passing by. Jacob had monitored the entrance to the general's tent, knowing that Prince Malik had re-entered, but had not come back out. Moving closer, he was met by immediate resistance when he stopped to strengthen the straps on both of his sandals. Dumbfounded, he was quickly picked up by two strong-armed guards posted nearby and moved a good forty meters ahead before his sandals hit the sand.

They caught him by such surprise, he had a hard time keeping loud, rude comments from streaming out of what should be a silent mouth.

"You move along in the night to your healer, Jacob the Mute. There will be no information passing from you to her this night. We know about you."

Several times he glanced back over his shoulder on the forty-minute trek back to their tent. Entering, he lifted the flap up in a huff, placing his hands on his hips. She turned, taking in right away his clearly displayed irritation.

"What do you have?" She turned, wiping the remnants off her fingertips onto a cloth.

He shook his head negatively.

"Nothing? Nothing at all? They are up to

something. I can feel it in the pit of my stomach. You need to get closer to them. Listen. Watch."

His head shook harder as he knelt down and drew two stick figures with swords.

"Oh, his guards moved you along? They are suspicious of you. Is that what you are trying to tell me? Did they say as much?"

He nodded yes several times.

"Shit. Okay. Damn, they are on to you. Which means they are on to me. Do you know where that sage is that Rano uses?"

He smiled, motioning with his head.

She dropped the cloth and Jacob the flap as they followed the moonlight through their part of camp. He halted, pointing inside a small tent. From its depths, a voice rang out, startling Jacob and Nofret.

"Stop lurking in those shadows, girl, and come in. I have a notion to speak with you and you have made me wait long enough. Time is running out. I grow impatient. Now get your bony ass in here."

***

Nofret walked in, letting her eyes adjust to the softly lit tent. Then she halted, feet embedded into the sand, unable to move any farther.

"Yes. It is me. Sit before I pin your ears back. Now let's get things straight right off the bat. I will not answer any of your questions just yet. You will listen and that's that. It is time. Again."

"Hello, Gerda. How have you been?"

"Smart ass still, I see. Sit. I have been well enough. But tired of seeing you time and again."

"Oh shit, Gerda, I feel really weird." Nofret sat quickly down. "I see things now. It is starting to come back. Unravel."

"It does every single time, dear. But we have to put a stop to it once and for all. We must."

"How? I want to. I really do. I know we have had this conversation before. Each and every time. By the way, how many has it been by now? Oh, don't answer. I am afraid to hear the number. What am I supposed to do?"

"Stop fighting it. Rano wants to move on and you need to move on. I'd think a future with Adam would be a bit more promising than repeating this over and again, missy."

A wan smile appeared and then turned into a full-fledged grin.

"This is not a time to be impertinent. I've got other things to do too, you know. Every time you refuse your true duty, you bring us all back. Don't you know that?"

That did it.

"Oh, my, I had not, well, I've not actually ever stopped long enough to think of anyone but myself."

Gerda nodded, watching closely.

"How many are here because of me and will finally have closure when I go back?"

"Adam, Rano, me, the queen and Pharaoh—and that's probably why he avoids you like the plague. At this juncture, he'd probably like to have you tortured and beheaded and just let the universe destroy him later. There are others as well. At this point, I can't keep track of them all. One of the guards, the master craftsman, you know he's got things to do too, and Clash. Is that a good enough list to begin with?"

"Clash too? Oh. Then I am affecting his life with Anne as well. Oh, my God. How come no one has explained this to me with such thoroughness before?"

"Oh, that's precious. I have. Every single time we sit in this tent, in the same desert, under the same sky and time of night and have this exact conversation."

"Oh damn."

"Yes, you even reply with that."

"I guess I'm not much of a healer here if I keep

dragging souls back to a time they want to exit from."

"Well, that's new."

She did not smile, standing. "I'll go now and spend some time up in the cave. Have I done that before? I don't remember if I have."

"No. You go do that. Take Jacob with you. He's one of us as well. He'd probably like to go back to where he was. Enjoying a conversation with a pleasant and charming tavern wench in Boston. Sure as shit smells from a donkey's ass, he was engaging her in a truly animated conversation. He probably would like to use his voice about now and give you a decided piece of his mind. Rightfully so."

"Okay, okay. I get it. Again." She exited the tent, scuffing up a large swirl of desert sand as her companion stood close by, waiting.

"I'm sorry, Jacob. I knew and pretended every time it did not matter. I'm going to fix this somehow."

Jacob's brows drew together in concern. He also had heard that before.

"What is it, Jacob? Do you have something to do?"

He nodded.

"Can you do it quickly?"

Again he nodded.

"Okay. Meet me in fifteen minutes. We are going up into the cave to spend some time before the battle." She turned to say something else, but he had already disappeared from sight.

As they met outside, Nofret watched Jacob hand a guard something rolled up but forgot to ask him what it was as they proceeded on together.

On their trek to the cave, she kept glancing down to see the torches of the camp and how it spread out for miles. Twenty minutes straight up and she finally halted as he lit a fire and settled his blanket to keep the scorpions at bay. She squatted down like a monk, folding her legs resembling an oasis lotus.

Her eyes fixed on the encampment below.

For twenty-four hours they sat, neither sleeping, as he kept watch. She did not utter a word as nightfall began. At last, she rose and rolled the blanket. "I'm ready, Jacob."

He nodded, following the goat trail back to the camp. She did not wonder if Rano would be concerned that she had not come to him last night. Tonight she would. She had to. At her tent, she opened the flap and set her things inside, nodded to Jacob, and then left.

It seemed strange to her that the horse was all prepared. It must have been for someone else. Or, had an unknown indeed been made aware of her last minute travel plans and their only passage was to come and make sure it was ready?

Now her mind was really beginning to engage.

She glanced up to the stars. "How do you know this? You must be pretty sorry to see me again. Well, this time I am going to work my hardest."

A roar of thunder echoed angrily across the nighttime sky as she ducked, then smiled. As she approached his tent, sliding quietly off and handing the reins over to one of the guards posted, he lifted the flap and she walked softly in. Rano's trained ears had already known, before he'd even turned around, that she had arrived.

"I did not come last night because I had to go up to the cave and think."

"It is okay."

She steered into his arms.

Suddenly, he had to wonder if it was he who had been holding her back. "You will stay the night."

She nodded, not disrobing him. Rather, she took his hand as they sat down on a pile of blankets. "When do you march?"

He pulled her closer, leaning back on his side.

"Tomorrow as the sun sets. We will meet them in the southern reaches on the following day. You will stay here. Do as I say, wife, I mean it."

Alas, they both knew better.

"I will remain with you, then, until early morning. We will not make love. I want you to remember more of me than just your lust for my body, Rano the Mercenary."

He polished off the wine and dropped the silver goblet into the sand. "Unless you change your mind during the night, healer."

She grinned, always loving that name, while tugging his head down to a kiss. "We shall see."

In minutes they were both sound asleep. As darkness gave away to a lightening sky, she opened her eyes and felt if her clothing was still in place. It was. Moving softly from his embrace, she stood to smooth it down.

"I will love you forever," she whispered. Then she raised the tent flap and walked towards the waiting guard and horse. Mounted, she glanced back only once, nodded thanks at his early morning duty, and then rode off.

Within minutes of departure, the entire encampment was up and awake. Men emerged, dressed in their battle tunics with gear prepared to deliver a decisive blow to their enemy. Moving through them as they assembled to march south to meet the Kush army, she felt shivers go up her spine.

Sliding off the mount, she handed the reins to Jacob. He walked the horse off toward where the others were corralled, tied the barrier, and returned.

She was deep in thought. "Well, now we wait. Did you eat? You are up early. I guess everyone is. You can feel it in the air, Jacob. Death. Death is coming."

Gerda's hand slid on top of her right shoulder. "Death and peace, healer. For some, it will be both."

Enlightening energy raced from her toes to her head

as she spun around to reply.

But there was no one else there except Jacob.

"Did I just imagine her?"

He nodded, pointing to the telltale footprints her sandals had made in the sand. Retreating from them both.

"I don't think I can stay here. I wonder if I may have a better advantage moving to higher ground. What do you think about that bluff?"

He shook his head sharply back and forth. But she was already ditching him, heading inside her tent as he closely followed.

"Jacob, I have to go. I can't wait here for word two days from now and wonder what the hell is going on."

"For all and damnation, girl. No, you cannot go. I repeat this every single time. Precisely at this moment. Yet you still refuse to listen. Stubborn as bloody hell and go anyway. If you do, it will distract him. Do you want that?"

Their forward progress halted immediately. He looked apprehensive. The very fact that he spoke, Nofret realized, repeating past warnings, and the fact that she was still going to go, had her wondering what to really do. No, she had to. The deliberation and decision were made and firm. No backing out now.

"I must. You stay here. You will be safer. Did you come with me all the other times?"

"Yes."

"Then stay. It will make a difference."

But as she left and began the climb up the rocky terrain, she knew he was right behind, close on her heels. It did not matter; she kept right on going. It was easy to locate the army at this height as they kept pace with the dust cloud down in the desert valley.

When they halted at nightfall to rest in the desert, eat and drink, she noticed no tents were put up. No fires were lit and silence filled the darkness. No conversation could be heard echoing up to them high on the hill.

She took out bread, pulled off a chunk and handed it to him and they ate and drank in silence. Both of their minds were locked into their own world. Nestling into a ball, head resting on her arms, she drifted off to sleep. Jacob was but a few feet away. As her lids dropped, she thought he was already asleep.

***

Later a boot nudged Jacob. Eyes opening, he watched a hand lower a scroll down beside his side. He turned his head quickly toward Nofret and back again. But the person had left quietly back into the dark night. Leaning up on one elbow, he glanced over at her sleeping form and waited a few minutes before unraveling the scroll and holding it up into the moonlight to read.

He smiled and folded it, tucking it inside his pouch. Then he went back to sleep.

***

As the heat of the sun beat down on them, they rose. Each disappeared for a few minutes before returning to eat and drink prior to their final trek. Nofet broke the silence. "We have not seen any of the Kush soldiers up this high. But I see tracks. They are not from wandering animals. They are from sandals. It must be that they have trackers up this high and soon enough they will head back down to where it is safer and report their findings. I don't think we need to worry about them spotting us. Those tracks must have been from yesterday before we arrived last night."

Jacob kept his mouth shut.

Throughout the day they kept pace until the sun was lowering into the desert and the large army finally stopped. The footsteps of the trackers headed up and out of sight as they spotted men Jacob recognized pointing over towards their area. They were posted sentries. She nodded, knowing full well those below knew they were up here. She was pleased that they were being left alone.

Stopping, crouching down and biting on a balled-up

fist, Nofret remained there silent.

"Are you okay?"

"I did it again." She kicked at a stone sending it flying over the path's edge.

"Yup, you sure have. You never learn, do you?"

"Apparently not. So mind if I ask what is next?"

"Does not matter in the least what I say now. I'm going to save my words. You will end up doing what you always do."

"I can't help myself. What's wrong with me? Is it all about him?"

"Nope, you are selfish. It's all about you."

She shrugged, having not recalled hearing those words from him before. But sure she had heard the others. "How far are we from the Valley of the Kings?"

He pointed in front of her nose. "There. We are practically on sacrilegious ground right now. If we even wanted to get there, it would involve us going down this steep hillside, into the valley, right through the heart of the army and up over that hill. It would take us probably all night and into tomorrow."

She nodded at his lengthy description. She liked a man that spewed out a good sentence. "Okay. Then let's go. Standing around like this means we are wasting precious time. I've got a plan and it is going to work."

"What?"

"If up to now most everything is status quo, then I know going there is not. So it's like I said—" She was already up and moving down the trail, eyeing the best way to cross the valley to the other side. "—get your ass in gear or you won't get back to that wench in Boston, England, Jacob the Mute."

All the way down he kept muttering, "I hope you know what the fuck you are doing. This can't be right. I should have tied you up back at the tent. Oh, I don't like this. It is not good."

Every word he uttered simply egged her further on. She turned, walking backward just before they hit the rear of the army, much to the amazement of several soldiers. But she kept on.

"First you would not speak for days. Now it is clear that I can't shut you up. Come on, old man, keep pace. A lot faster steps and a lot fewer words would work for me about now."

She spun around as a massive wall of chest smacked her right in the nose. "Ow, that hurt! Step aside, I say. I am on important business for your General Rano. I am Nofret Qalhata the Healer."

The soldier paused, looking at his men, perplexed. Then he stepped aside, allowing the unlikely twosome to begin their long trek through their massive numbers.

She did not care as she wove through hundreds of them if Jacob was still with her or not. She'd never turned around again to seek him out. When they reached the other side it was dark. But the sky was bright enough to light their way.

"You doing okay back there? Are you even still back there? I've not heard you in hours."

He laughed, catching up with her. Then he stopped to take a much-needed piss. "You hardly knew and did not care. But just so you know, I am fine. You want to stop for a minute, or keep moving?"

"No and no. I have a plan. Let me ask you how many times I've repeated this little maneuver?"

"Zilch. So I must admit I'm intrigued and actually plan on observing through the duration."

She smiled to no one but herself. "I think I calculated the distance right. We should be well out of reach of the battle but close enough to watch it from over there. I could see from that ridge we crossed before sunset. That location was partially vacated. I am thinking only soldiers are guarding it now and the slaves have been moved to a different location until this is over. Again."

"Well, toots, we are soon to find out."

She let that slide. Onward they trekked throughout the night and into the better part of the following morning before the pyramids loomed larger and larger. She saw that she'd been right as they watched a small band of armed soldiers on camels trot out towards them. Suddenly Nofret was confused. It appeared to her as if they had been expecting her and Jacob all along. For in tow they had two extra. Just as they arrived, the beasts were commanded to kneel.

"Get on," was all the conversation she received. Her gut instinct was that she had fucked up even more. Otherwise, how the hell would they have known?

"Seems as if they were awaiting our arrival, Jacob. I think I've done something wrong. Yet you said we had not done this before. Could I have been with someone else another time because you were someplace else?"

"That is correct and no. I can pretty much recite your exact moves and words as if I wrote the script myself. You know, perhaps this time the gods are working with you and not against. Maybe they are just tired of seeing you in this era."

She glanced over at his amused look and relaxed, staring straight ahead. The final resting place in the Valley of the Kings of Thutmose II and many others finally came into clear view.

"Someday, his son will be there as well. One of the last ones."

"Yes. Before the looters get to them all."

She slid off the camel and stood. "Now I am not sure what to do." She wove around in a circle, trying to decide on a direction. Then she halted, realizing that the soldiers and camels had disappeared.

"What the hell? Where did they go? Did you see?"

He glanced around. "No. That is strange, Nofret.

What are you thinking? Feeling? Take your time. This is a very important moment."

Head lowered and eyes closed, she breathed a steady rhythm in and out, feeling and listening to all thoughts around her. "That I need to pee. Then maybe I will think better." She grinned, walking behind a bush. Finished, she lowered her tunic and returned. She tapped him on the right shoulder but appeared on his left, startling him.

"Stop being naughty. Did that little excursion exercise your brain enough to give any ideas?"

"Yes." They both glanced towards the large opening and tunnel inside the massive pyramid. "Let's go inside. It will be cooler and we can eat and drink. Maybe that's where they disappeared to."

But there was not a soul to be found in the chamber they entered.

"I can't even find tracks from them. Oh my God, Jacob, I feel so strange. It must be getting close because I don't normally feel this very way. In fact, I do not recall ever feeling this way. I'm a bit frightened." She rubbed the skin on both of her arms as numbness wove its way up.

"This is spooky. I've never been in a pyramid before when it still housed tombs and rooms not yet sealed. Oh my, look at the drawings above this entrance. You have to come here now. It is Rano. Oh God… yes. Now I know I have been in here before. I think."

"Do you feel it? Hear the voices off in the distance? The battle has begun."

Nofret lowered her head and looked at him, feeling sheer panic grow inside of her in a split second. "Yes," she stuttered out back to him. "I do."

For hours they listened as the ground beneath their feet rumbled with the vibration of thundering hooves and chariot wheels as the battle raged. Neither spoke as outside from high above, the vultures and ravens circled in anticipation of fresh flesh and blood to gorge themselves on. The screams and yells of men fighting and dying echoed through the walls of the great pyramid.

Nofret sat down on a gold bench and felt the coldness of the mineral penetrate through her clothing.

"How long?"

"Any time now."

"Will you help me?"

"No, you have to do this on your own. But, if you need guidance, glance at me. Hell, yell at me and ask me if you should or should not do something. As long as I don't lay a hand on you and halt you physically, we are okay."

"You were with me last time and the time before that and I can see your mouth moving, yelling at me. But, I don't know what you are saying." She looked down at her left hand. "Is it starting to get see-through?"

"You hang on. Listen. Something else has occurred and here the soldiers come. Get prepared. Every time you see this, it is like viewing with fresh eyes."

She had no idea what he was talking about. His mouth was moving but no words reached her ears. Suddenly she saw what was causing all the commotion over Jacob's head as four men carried on a slab the lifeless, bloodied body of their great leader, Rano.

Gasping, rushing to stand, she hurried over to Rano, utterly horrified. His tunic and robe were saturated with blood. "Quick! Put him down!" She glanced up, momentarily locking eyes with Jared as he set her bags down hastily. They both opened up and the contents spilled out. Swiftly, she reached for ointment.

"Take that robe off. Here, you." She pointed to a soldier. "Give me your knife. I will rip it quick so as to not cause him undue pain." She finished, throwing the bloody clothes aside as everyone inside the tomb of the pyramid closed in around her and Rano.

That's when she saw Jared holding Rano's sword

just as Rano's blood squirted, splattering out all over her face and eyes. Hastily she cupped a large amount of the green salve onto a palm and filled the wound. He moaned as her heart filled with pure agony, trying to absorb all his pain. Willing it to become her very own.

"My woman and wife. You are here. As this was prepared for me, for this day, I will be at my final rest. But only if you let me go." Rano's eyes fluttered, closed and opened again.

She leaned down, pressing her lips to his as tears streamed down her face onto his cold skin.

"Be brave, Nofret. No matter what. I will always love you. Now, we must part."

She clutched one of his hands tightly with a bloody one and yelled out in agony. The tormented sound echoed around the large chamber as her gaze, through tear-streaked eyes, saw others already down on one knee.

"Malik, bring me that sword!"

He could not disobey her. She took it from his hand and laid it on top of Rano's cold body. Moving his hands rapidly, she forced them to grasp it tightly along the handle. Momentarily her mind shut down. Her hands now rested on top of his, her own head lowered.

A beautiful lapis stone dislodged and popped into her hand. She turned it over, staring at it, crying, as one other came out.

She stopped.

Reaching down, she took some salve off his drying wound, put some on each of the stones and placed them back where they truly belonged. Somewhere in the recesses of her mind she was aware that when it dried they would adhere.

For an hour she sat with him until his body was stiff.

As if in a dream, she felt a hand press onto her shoulder and she raised her eyes to Malik's. Standing, ripping a section of her own tunic off, Nofret placed it over Rano's closed eyes and then looked again at Malik.

"Come with me."

She glanced around the room. All others were gone except two guards and servants from his household. They would take care of him properly, she knew.

"Please make sure no one removes those stones."

They nodded as she passed through the chamber, noticing that items of his were being moved in. That quick? How could that be? Glancing down at her feet, she was momentarily horrified to see that they were not touching the dirt below. Slowly she raised a fist and bit on it, not feeling the sensation of pain.

"You did it."

"What?" Her voice was hardly recognizable, even to her own ears.

"You did not take the stones. That was what caused him to always seek you out. He needed you to love him enough to leave all of him behind. That included them."

"I was the one that stole them when he lay dying?"

"Yes, out of love, Nofret. You loved him very much and he you."

"Can you still see me?"

Malik smiled, taking her by the arm. Above them, the sun hit a global opening, producing a glorious sunbeam that shone brightly upon them.

"Yes, I can see you and I've got you now. At last."

Then suddenly, angry voices were growing louder and louder.

"There they are!"

As Sam and Adam turned toward the growing sound, he grabbed her hand and the bag on the floor as they sped out of the museum and through their emergency exit, vanishing into the night. The guards were fast on their heels when they hit the outside.

***

"What the hell? Where did they go?"

"Shit, we need to get back in there and see if anything was taken." The museum guards quickly returned to that section, checking over every square inch thoroughly. "It all seems in order. That's strange."

One pointed over at the life-size statue of Rano the Mercenary. "I don't recall that sword standing out so much. I wonder if it is a copy and that's what was taken?" He glanced quickly around the silent room. "I'll make sure to ask the curate and verify its authenticity just in case. I'll get him on the phone straight away."

"I think it was replaced with a replica earlier this week when you were on vacation. Yeah, check with him and make sure. I think we scared them out just in time. I'll go back to the control room and make sure all the monitors are working. You do a door-to-door sweep and keep your radio close in case you find anything at all out of sorts."

But they found nothing wrong other than a magnificent addition to the great statue of Rano the Mercenary. His sword was mighty indeed and gloriously encased with gems and jewels that no one could explain, but they later proved to be authentic. Nor could any discern anything else amiss. Including the cameras, which had malfunctioned for eleven minutes.

Chapter Eleven

They both laughed all the way back to the Nefertiti Hotel. Finally, he slowed down to her panting words. "I am so happy to be done there! How did you know? You have a lot to tell me, mister. How many women did you indulge with? What did you do with your time?"

He pulled her close and kissed her. He knew what would happen next even if he'd never seen it before. She was going to feel his soul leave her body soon. It could be tonight or it could be in three days. But it was going to happen. She needed to know right now, remember right now, the love they shared here before mourning Rano.

Releasing her, he took her by the hand and led them away from the hotel door and up toward a chapel. She glanced up, stumbling slightly. As he righted her, both laughed. They were headed directly into a small church.

As soon as they opened up the doors, she was sitting in a small boat while he rowed them through Meuse. A lovely canal through the old City of Brugge. She dipped her hand into the cool water and splashed him slightly. He raised a brow.

"They say the chocolate here is molded into several different styles. I think we'd find something for both our tastes and desires."

He grinned and kept rowing.

"Looks like, by our attire, we are in somewhat older times. I truly hope we are between all the wars and well after all the plagues."

His smile grew. He loved having her back with him. Just him.

"Did you lose your tongue in Egypt?"

"No. Just listening to your voice, Sam. I missed just

hearing you."

She moved gingerly. The boat was sturdy enough but rocked, precariously close to allowing water to spill in.

"Careful."

She kept on creeping until she was kneeling on the bench in front of him as the oars came inside the boat.

They both released a contented sigh at the same time.

"I can see it on your face. Are you feeling a bit strange?"

"Yes. Am I that transparent to you, Adam? What is wrong with me?"

He kissed her lips softly and pulled away. "He is releasing your soul now. I have no idea how long that takes. But you will be solemn while it happens. Or, so the gypsy advised as well as Gerda."

"I feel it now. I look at you one minute and I want to crawl into your skin and the next I want to be alone."

He did not fully understand but was willing to try. "I won't interfere with this process. But I will stay close in case you need me."

She nodded as a tear formed and dropped. "Bugga. I don't like feeling this soft."

He chuckled. "Don't suppress it. That is all the advice I'm allowed to give. Oh yeah, and do not try and drown it out with alcohol or a good smoke was the other."

"Shit. Who comes up with these bloody rules anyway? Some eunuch with no body parts to know the pleasures we experience?"

He lost it, laughing out loud. "You do come out with really interesting sentences sometimes."

She wiped the wetness from her cheeks. "So while I was busy doing other things, tell me what you were up to."

He shrugged his shoulders. "Ah, you know a bit of tactical maneuvering and all." He knew now was not the time to tell her that he was the twin of her Egyptian mercenary lover.

"What about the women? You telling me you did not have any kind of enjoyment? The man of mistresses?"

"Why are you pushing this? I happen to know that before you two were officially acknowledged as man and wife by the Pharaoh, that you spent a few times in his tent. At least once I know you had intercourse with him. Hell, Sam, you two were in love. Even I recognized that and had to try and reconcile for a spell why I was there. I was sure it was not just to watch it happen and be so punished by it."

"Nice diversion. No need to answer. You are right. I'll shut up about that area henceforth and vow it shall never be brought up again. How can we be accountable for something that was going to happen before this happened, right?"

"Well said, my dear."

"Oh, sod off."

"Now that's better."

The dock attendant secured the rowboat as Adam stepped out, turning to extend his hand to her. She clasped on to it so tight he could feel it up his arm.

"Sorry, really did not feel like falling in right now. I'm hungry for some good old-fashioned food. Oh look, see? It's like I said earlier, there are chocolate concoctions to suit all desires."

He stood in front of the lavishly displayed store window lined with row upon row of chocolates in all sizes, shapes, and color. "Oh, I see the ones. Ah yes, the very ones. Look, all I can say is a set of those would do me well except I like the real thing and they belong to you."

Glancing at her face quickly, he stopped his comical banter when he noticed her discomfort. "Come on. Over there is a nice little restaurant. I see quite a few ladies and gents going in."

She adjusted her plumed hat and took his arm. "I think we are somewhere between the Great Wars. It looks like down a few of the alleys is still some rubble."

He nodded as they were situated at a nice table by the windows.

"Please just order for me. Do we know where we are staying?" The waiter approached as Adam spoke to him and then looked out at what she was glancing towards and realized she was gazing awkwardly at her own reflection in the window. The silence grew between them.

As their food was brought over he noticed she hardly ate. He knew the whole process of her much-needed release from Rano, and his release from her was taking place. Paying the bill, he rose and extended his arm, bringing them out into the old cobbled streets.

"I bet a good bike ride would lift your spirits. How about tomorrow? I can locate one with a bell and basket and set you off on a proper jaunt. Some time alone. What do you think?"

Her eyes lifted in genuine happiness. "Yeah, that would help. Thank you. Is this where we are staying?"

He opened up an exterior door and motioned her inside ahead of him while producing a key with leather ID attached. "Yes, it says so right here."

She jabbed him in the ribs as they walked up a flight of steps. He unlocked another door and pushed it open while they both viewed the small apartment.

It was cozy with plenty of windows. He twisted on a light switch, and the bulb came to life, but barely produced a dim return. Sam was at the window looking out over one of the many canals in Brugge.

"It's lovely here."

He glanced about. "One bedroom, Sam. I'm sorry. I can sleep quite comfortably on the sofa."

She took his hand as he stepped beside her. "I don't think you should. I need to feel your life as his leaves mine. I know that's selfish, but I can't help it."

He squeezed her hand. "I've seen something."

"Already? We just got back. Where and when do we leave?"

He put a hand to the window pane, feeling the coolness. "Not you, just me. I leave tomorrow."

"Oh."

"It's for a good reason, I'm sure."

"Perhaps you are right. I'll know when it's time for me soon enough. Do you know if you will be coming back here?"

He shook his shoulders. "Can't really tell at this point what will happen after that. I wish I had more to give."

She moved away from the window, sitting down on a chair and unlacing her boots. The leather was soft, and she let her hands weave over the top. "I had a pair something like this back at the cottage. That seems like thousands of years ago now. I think those planners upstairs know exactly what they are doing. No sense in you being around a mope like me while this all transpires. Good move on their part, I'd say."

He stood back, feeling a bit uneasy. This was new for them both at this point.

She turned. "Well, I need that kind bloke that was so patient with me back in New Orleans to unbutton me. Tomorrow I'll go and see if I can secure simpler clothing or hire a part-time maid."

His fingers fumbled with the tiny buttons. "Or get a few gowns where they button down the front. These are a royal pain in the ass."

She laughed as he nudged her forward toward the room. He could see her washing in the tiny bathroom and then wiping her face with a cloth. He watched her walk back into the room and climb straight into bed.

"I'm not sure I can sleep in this after the bedding I had back in Egypt or at the cottage. I am spoiled, Adam, that's for sure."

He walked into the bathroom and leaned down on the ceramic sink, running the water and splashing his face before glancing up for a few seconds at his reflection. He shook the uncertainty from his head. But not from his heart.

***

Moving the pillow to the center of the bed, Sam fluffed it several times and settled onto it. Turning the switch off, he got in as the darkened room filled with streaming moonlight.

"Already feels like we've lived together in a hundred lifetimes, Adam."

The back of his hand slid softly down one cheek as she kissed it. He leaned in, touching his lips softly to hers and pulling her onto his chest. She listened intently to the steady beat of his heart and the rhythm of his breathing, allowing both to soothe her tired mind, body, and spirit into a beautiful, deep sleep.

She was so glad someone upstairs had planned on one bedroom and not two. For if there had been two, he would have been the gentleman and insisted on being in the other one, knowing her pending condition. Together they drifted off to sleep.

As she turned over in the morning, her hand instantly went to his spot. One eye opened, followed by a second. He was not there. "Adam?"

No answer.

She glanced over, frowning. His clothes were gone from the chair. He had left her already. Lying back down in bed, she fell back asleep. When she woke, she rolled over and glanced at the small wind-up clock, which displayed nine-thirty. A soft knock slightly rattled the door. Rising and walking over, she moved up on tiptoes and peered out through the keyhole. It was a woman she had not known before. At least she did not think so.

"Yes?"

"Ms. Arnesen, I'm Lucy. I know your gentleman

has left for business. He stopped into our company this morning and has contracted me to come and assist you twice daily should you require it."

She opened up the door. "I sure do. Especially with my dresses. I was going to do that myself this very morning. He's a thoughtful man." She closed it. "Would you be kind and advise me on where I can get a pot of tea and breakfast? Something close by. I am not in the mind yet to wander off too far until I take care of a few things."

Lucy grinned, stepping farther into the room. "Yes, I will write down places you can visit while you are alone. I have already stopped at the bike shop on the corner. When you are ready, they will fit you with a fine model. Many are new. So few survived the Great War. But you will be right at home here in Brugge. Almost all of us ride. It is just a lot easier to get around with the small lanes and cobbles. Plus, petrol prices are more than most of us can afford."

Cobbles. Her mind went to 2015 and the Tour of Flanders. It was one of her favorite one-day professional cycling classics. It was housed every year from this very location in Brugge.

"Miss?"

She spun around, facing her new acquaintance. "I am so sorry, Lucy. Please call me Samantha. I'd like it very much if you could come in the evenings around eight to help me get out of these dresses. Pretty as they are, I really need your assistance."

"If you are not here long and want more ease in your clothing, I can recommend a shop two blocks down that may have a few dresses in your size. They open later today. I've seen a few in their storefront window that have back zippers. All the rage and fresh in from the fashion pages of Paris."

She actually felt the smile starting deep within. "Zippers, you say?"

"Yes. They are all the talk now here in Brugge."

"Well then, I'll stop in this morning. Previously, you were trying to gain my attention. I apologize for woolgathering. Is that the list?"

"Yes. There is a lot in this general vicinity. Let me recommend the purchase of an umbrella. Although it is warmer now, it rains frequently here in the spring. I also listed a few markets where you can stock up if you get tired of eating out. The agency's name and address are on there as well. I am only a few minutes away."

"Great. What is your rate so I can pay you now?"

She put up her hand. "No need. Your gentleman paid for several weeks. If you depart sooner let us know and the difference will be returned."

"Excellent and you don't have to do that. Let's just call it a bonus that's between you and I, shall we? There are times when I just decide to move on and take the next train someplace. I will leave word at your office. But you keep the difference should there be one. I much appreciate your help and all the detailed information. You have already done me a great service."

Sam opened up the door for her, smiling as she left. No further small talk was needed. Enough was enough. She grabbed her reticle and looked inside. As usual, it was filled with plenty of the local currency. Belgian francs. So she slid it up her wrist, placed the key inside and closed it.

Humming an Egyptian tune, she left and was outside in short order. She stopped to glance up, the warmth of the sun's rays penetrating to her soul. Yes, she concluded. It was indeed a fine early spring day in Belgium.

Crossing those very famous cobbles, she felt a vigor in her step as she found the shop and engaged the clerk. Indeed, they had a spiffy black bike complemented with a bell and basket. How dandy.

"I shall keep this for at least a week unless my plans change. Just as a precaution, I will pay you for two weeks up front in case you do not see me." She filled out the verification card and signed it. "Will this be enough?"

"Indeed it will. Good thing you are paying for two. Later this week the racers are in town and the streets will be a throng of bustling activity. My supply will dwindle. I may not have rentals at the end of this week."

"Racers? You mean the Tour of Flanders racers? You see I am not from here. But from England and a big fan."

"Your accent gave you away, madam." He grinned.

Sam thought he was quite a nice man and a bit on the handsome side. Amusing enough was that his wife kept glancing out from behind a curtain keeping an eye on them both.

"What is the race route? Where from Brugge do they leave?"

"The center. Where we are right now. If you want to come and stand outside on Saturday, my wife and I would be happy to hold you a spot so you can watch them. They do a few laps through before heading out on the actual course."

"Oh, I will be here. I'd love that. Can I bring anything to celebrate? It would be my pleasure."

He laughed at her enthusiasm. "Anything you wish. We will supply paper cups. No sense in having anything finer than that."

"How old are your children?"

"Eight and ten and yes, of course, they like chocolate. Especially the pastries."

She nodded. "I shall bring wine for us grown-ups and goodies then for them. If I do not see you before, I will see you on race day. What time?"

"Earlier the better. We actually do that so we secure the best spots right in front of the shop. If we do not, then we lose out and watch from the upper windows. That's no fun."

"Wonderful. Thanks." She waved, mounted the bike, lifted the hem of the dress up a little, and pedaled off. She had no particular route in mind and just kept going until she stopped to let a lorrie pass. Glancing over, she saw people coming out of a small alley carrying large totes overflowing with exposed vegetable greens and fresh bread. Yeah, that was her direction.

Following tiny local signs, she stopped in wonder, gazing at the thriving marketplace next to the Belfry of Brugge and The Basilica of the Holy Blood. Jumping off, she walked the bike the rest of the way before resting it against a gas lamppost not in use yet. Then she started maneuvering through other people gathered to shop.

Stalls were filled with needed staples of nutritional value and delicious pastries that were not, Sam noticed. Eventually, she had the basket full, retrieved the bike then rode back to her temporary digs and unloaded it all. That finished, she took what was needed and went downstairs.

Back outside and on the bike, she started out again, this time with a small picnic already in that lovely, tidy basket. Weaving over the famous cobbles, her energy level rose as her muscles balked at the excessive pedal strokes.

She spoke out loud to no one. "I must be getting soft. Or need more gears than this." She laughed, continuing on.

Because Brugge was referred to as the Venice of the North, she had no trouble finding a beautiful bridge to cross. Breathless, she lowered both boots to the ground as she moved off the bike, setting it against a building. She then located a vacated bench and ate lunch. Relaxing, she watched a steady succession of boats and barges come into view before disappearing up the waterway.

She glanced to the heavens, speaking softly. "This is so beautiful. I'm not happy you took Adam away, but if you had to put me someplace where I needed reflective time, this works." She smiled into the fluffy white clouds floating by.

On her way back, as the sun set, the streets came alive with musicians playing mixtures of waltzes, polkas, and even very Parisian music. Setting the bike inside the building, she went back out and just walked until she came to Damme.

Turning, she crossed over one of the canal bridges and came back along the opposite path, stopping along the way at a café to sip tea and watch people stroll by. Rising, she paid the waiter and continued, heading upstairs before realizing she had forgotten to stop at the dress shop. What time was it?

She glanced at the small wind clock. It showed eight o'clock. As if on cue, Lucy's knock came directly after.

"Come on in. Perfect timing. I just got back. I was so fascinated by this area I lost track of time on my walk."

"My apartment is just across the street. I was watching for you."

"I'm sorry you had to do that. You probably have other things you may prefer to be doing. I forgot today to stop in that shop. But I will tomorrow before I leave. Can I see your place from up here?"

"Yes." Lucy was unbuttoning her dress. "Right across, see? I left a light lit."

"Indeed I do. But now I am having a thought. Should I find a few dresses of use that I can get into and out of on my own, I will not need your services. In exchange, would you be free to give me more advice on where to go and what to do outside of Brugge? I would love to take full advantage of my bike."

"But he paid me for so many more days."

Sam scoffed, waving both hands. "Not an issue. Having a local tell me things I'd not know is worth a lot more than you having to bother coming here for only a few minutes in the morning and evening to do these silly buttons."

She had finished. "Absolutely I can. Tell me what you are interested in and I'll bring a new list with me tomorrow morning. If you have left, I will slide it under the door. Will that work?"

"Perfect. I'd like to know more about Damme and other towns near here. I like to ride, Lucy, so if it is fifteen kilometers or more I'd be happy to jaunt off. I also like history, architecture, art and old churches. Now don't go laughing at me, I know what you are going to say. But this is Brugge!"

"I can't help it. I enjoy your enthusiasm. I'll set you up with an interesting list. Some areas are still being rebuilt after the Great War. But there are places the Germans actually did not destroy for its architectural grandeur. I will take care of this and see you in the morning."

"Thanks very much. I look forward to what you come up with. Have a good night." She smiled and closed the door.

Sam washed up and went to the window to watch the people stroll by, feeling better. She opened one as a cool breeze wafted in off the canal below. Turning and climbing into bed, she laid a weary head and body down on the pillow. A quick roll-over left her improving mood diminished as she threw the second pillow out of sight onto the floor. It was the noise of the street below that proved to be a needed distraction, finally shutting her brain down so she could fall asleep.

After Lucy left the next morning, Sam sat down with a pot of tea and reviewed the list. Cool stuff. She had definitely a future in the travel industry if she ever wanted one. Glancing at the clock and then jumping up, she quickly washed the dishes and left them to dry on a wooden rack before dashing from the apartment to the shop. Lucy had been right. It took Sam only a few minutes to find the shop door.

"Hello, Miss. What can we do for you?"

"Well, I hear that you may just have what all the ladies around are buzzing about. The new style from Paris and it involves dresses and zippers. Would you happen to have one that may fit a lady of my size?"

The dressmaker eyed her. "I think I do. Why don't you come with me to the back and see what we can come up with?"

One hour later Sam left the shop with one of the shopkeeper's sons close in tow. They carried five boxes between them up to her apartment, where she slipped a sizable tip into his hands. The door could not close fast enough for her to begin opening the boxes. At the shop she had the clerk help her to change into one. Now all that was needed was some snacks and her bike. There was exploring to be done.

Taking her reticule and umbrella just in case, she grabbed the premade picnic and loaded up her bike. Forty minutes of steady riding later had her stopping beside a field and glancing around. A happy smile lit her face as she spotted a graveyard and spire of a ruined church dating back to the year 504.

Oh, how she longed for Father G about now.

Hopping off, she walked the bike, finding the perfect picnic spot. Setting it down on the grass, she took the food and drink and enjoyed this tranquil, peaceful location.

Softly the words just came out. "I've not heard your voice, Rano, for a few days. Are you done with me and now chasing those wenches up in the heavens?" Lips quivered as the first tear dropped. Then, quickly, several more, until a steady stream flowed.

"I don't understand. I let you go. Why do I feel so empty without you? Are we not finished with business?"

She slumped slightly, crossing both hands over her heart.

"Open your eyes, woman."

She shook her head, placing it in her hands, and then brought her legs up, tucking them under her chin.

"Open them."

"No. I am not going to see you. You are gone. I am here. I do not hear you."

A warm breeze lifted her hair and removed her braid. It sprang to life, swirling around before lying loosely down her back. She pulled it to one side in a bunch, her eyes opening slowly. There on the ground, right beside her left hip, rested the gold hair thread.

She gasped.

"You are releasing me?"

She picked it up. As it dangled she tried to smile but was in so much anguish. "You kept part of it, this is only half."

A powerful bright light surrounded him as he knelt before her, raising his palm. She lifted one of her own toward him. His other hand gently caressed her cheek as all the wetness simply evaporated. Their hands touched as, mesmerized, she felt a lightning bolt of intense energy surge through her being.

"Yes. It is time for us both. I have loved you throughout the old. Now, my brother will love you throughout the new. As our souls move on, my lovely, you will heal. I will heal. Eventually, only bits will be in your memory. It is time."

He released her hand as the sun's rays diminished behind a passing cloud. He faded, disappearing in seconds. Struggling, she reached out into the air and then stopped. Tying the cord back into her hair, she curled into a ball and broke down sobbing.

Racks of pain seared her soul. But slowly her heart began to mend. Heal. Just as he said. It left her weak as she unfurled and reached into a slit pocket, producing a cotton hanky to wipe her eyes and blow her nose.

Then her mind went blank and nothing followed but silence.

It was welcoming.

Time passed unnoticed until she realized the sounds of the approaching night were fast upon her. Sitting up farther and crossing her legs, she started to gain control. Lifting her eyes up from the green grass and glancing around, she felt bereft as images of Rano quickly disappeared from her vision. She closed them tight and let the coolness of the stone against her back weave around her, bringing her slowly back to reality.

Not a soul was around at this hallowed place. She rose, grabbed her hat, put it back on, took the picnic bag and walked back to her bike. On her short journey through the graveyard, a warming inside her soul started to take place. Yes, his exit was painful. Years of being pent up in there due to her own selfishness. "Oh, Rano. I am so sorry I held you for so very long. Find peace, my love."

A cool wind lifted her hat up off her head and swirled it around before dropping it to the unkempt grass a few yards beyond. As she leaned down to pick it up, she saw his face looking right at her. He did not say a word but smiled. It was that special smile that spoke volumes about how he felt toward her when no more words would be allowed. It was a love that spanned time and space, just like her love with Adam. She reached a finger out magically just as did he. In that one brief instant, they touched.

Then both were free.

For several minutes she absorbed it all until he passed from her thoughts completely. It was as if someone from the twenty-second century had taken the motherboard out of her brain and deleted most of him from it. Shaking her head at the sound of children laughing in the distance, Sam walked back to her bike and sat with one foot resting on the ground and one on a pedal as she looked around.

"Of course there is no one here but me." She

smiled, pushed off and started the journey back to the apartment. A soothing breeze was at her back now. Yes, she felt whole again.

"Now, Lord Griffin, where shall I find you? Do you think any of you up there could lend me a hand now that I've done right by us all? You owe me for finally smartening up, you know." She giggled while reaching the cobbles at the outskirts of Brugge. Then she took her sweet time putting the bike away. On the slow climb up the stairs, she suddenly broke out in a dash, hoping that someone had told him the good news and he would be waiting for her when the door opened.

A brief flicker of sadness passed through her when it was flung open and the rooms reviewed. He was not there. *Oh well*, she thought to herself. Tomorrow was the race and she was eager for this day to pass so that the rest of her life, wherever that was going to be, could commence.

Then it dawned on her. Feeling bold, she made one more request. "Oh, shit. Can you also do me one more favor and not shuffle me from here tomorrow? If you could make it the day after. I want to see the race."

She laughed softly, hoping she had not pissed the people upstairs off. But in truth, she really did want to be here. To be that close to the racing and disappear would just not be fair. "Please?" was added as an afterthought.

Chapter Twelve

"You've been seen all around Brugge's countryside. Do you know what some of the locals in the neighborhood have taken to calling you?"

"Yes, that damn crazy dame from England. I rather like it." She grinned ear to ear. "Oh, don't say it. I do not want you to ruin my mood. Look, here comes the first group. I am so excited I can hardly stay inside my skin."

"Yes, stop flailing your arms. Or you are going to do bodily damage to my entire family."

Sam laughed a bit too loud, her enthusiasm getting in the way. Glancing down, she made sure her boots were not extending over the curb as the gust of heavy wind came by them with the first group of cyclists.

"How I wish I could ride like they do."

"That would be scandalous and you know it. They will be by three more times. But not for about thirty minutes. Now, where is that wine?"

She reached behind into the bag and produced the bottle and cork. "Where is your husband? Oh, I see him. I'll get him to open this." Mary was smiling at Sam's enthusiasm. Since arriving, this quarter of the neighborhood had lightened up at the wonderful atmosphere she brought every place she went.

"No need, we are women. Surely together we can get it opened. We don't have to worry about the kids. Look at them filling their faces at this time of day with those treats you bought. Which will bring a tongue lashing from my lovely mother-in-law, I am quite sure."

"Well, I may add, look at us for drinking this early in the day before most people have had a proper pot of tea."

They giggled, heads together, as the cork was

removed with a thud and flew across the narrow street. "Oh, my, good thing they had already passed. Look, here he comes now with those parents of his. Quick, fill my cup so I can drink it and have another. Then it could actually be possible that I may like them more."

"Oh, I got that a few days ago. They are not your favorite apples in the bunch."

"Sour grapes are more like it. There, I feel the warmth. That's much, much better. Now drink and fill me up."

Sam hid a smile behind her hand as they indeed descended upon them. "You seem to have the best spots already taken, I see." She shook her head in disdain. "I guess I could go upstairs inside of the shop and watch from the windows."

Sam nudged Mary.

"Oh, Mother, my apologies. I got caught up in the moment. By all means, have my spot. I am a few inches taller and can see over your head." She moved back, grabbing Sam by the arm and giving it a mighty tug. If she had to give up her spot to see them, so was Sam.

"I would have bit your hand if I had known what you were up to."

"Shush, she has the ears of a predatory mountain lion on the prowl in the wilds of Africa."

They chuckled. "I just saw Arthur trying to hide his grin. I think he enjoys my having a poke of fun with his plump, old, nosy, meddling mother."

"You did not miss any adverbs there, did you? I noticed they are both good to the kids. I've seen that with my own two eyes. Where are your parents?"

"Abroad in Germany. They have a joint business. With these grumblings of unrest making headlines they decided to go back. It is time to sell and cut their losses."

"You are German?" The concern could not be kept from Sam's voice. She was fully aware of what would transpire in the next twenty-plus years.

"Nope, Austrian and French. But all the same." She touched her shoulder fondly. "I know, Sam. Thanks for your thoughts."

"I'm glad to hear that. Not that I would not like you all the same. I know how Brugge is somewhat of a melting pot with Germans having stayed here after the Great War and all. You did not even sound like you had that kind of an accent and your name is not German. Anyway, I digress. How's your stomach? Time for a pastry to absorb your early morning courage?"

"Yeah, I'll have that chocolate one. Can't seem to keep them off my lips nor what eventually forms on my hips."

"May I recommend renting a bike for a day and coming along with me? It would ruin any extra calories from having the idea of settling where you prefer they do not. Besides, I visited Damme the other day and was taken aback. It is so beautiful. Surely you must have been before."

She nodded. "Yes, we have. Walked and taken a picnic last summer." She leaned closer. "I heard somewhat bizarre gossip late yesterday. Some passers-by at the cemetery saw a woman curled up in a ball crying her eyes out. Those that came across her did not even bother to see if she was sick or needed assistance. I guess they thought she was crazy. Some people. Willing to tell a good tall tale. Indeed, I know these two blokes. They are always in their cups before our eyes are even open in the morning. I put quick work to their story. Told them if I heard it about the neighborhood, I'd tell both their mothers where they really go every night after work. It is sure as hell not to chapel to pray."

Sam smiled, realizing the special message. "You are indeed a good sort, regardless of what she may think." Her finger pointed to the mother-in-law. "I wish I was here longer. I'd like to get to know you a lot better."

"Yes, you are in transit, I know. When will your man come back and get you, or are you leaving here to meet him? You seem well enough to travel on now, don't you think?"

"I'm really curious about you. What do they call your type?" They both got closer.

"Watchers."

"I think I read long ago there are two types. You are clearly of the warm-hearted version. You do not assist like I do? But observe and lend a hand as needed?"

"That's right. There is a pecking order so to speak. You are pretty close to the top of the pyramid, Sam."

She watched her closely, having chosen that particular word for a purpose.

"Pyramid. You knew."

"We have to know what we will to help you when the time is right."

"Do you know where Adam is?"

"He's here."

"What?"

"You did hear me. He is here. I could not out and out tell you. Against protocol and all. You had to ask me first for me to give you a correct answer. It was not possible for you to heal properly if he was to stay with you. Would you honestly say you would still have broken down like you did if he was?"

She shook her head roughly, polishing off her wine. "No. I would have buried it. Where exactly is he right now?"

"At the Basilica of the Holy Blood in the Old Center. He did have to take care of some of his own personal business. That is why he returned from the East with you here. I think you two basically punch your own time travel cards."

She handed her the bag and bottle along with the

remaining goodies and nodded, lifting her dress hem and bolting quickly across the cobbles. Glancing nervously, she half expected one of the abundantly placed police guards would halt her progress. Waving over a shoulder, quickly she disappeared into a throng of people on the opposite side of the street.

Not giving a bloody damn what she was leaving behind, she rushed on. Lucy could have it all if she so chose. A brick wall of gatherers halted her forward progress. Would these people ever get out of her way? She was growing impatient, giving a good shove to a tall gent that seemed to want to block her as he tipped and spilled his beer onto his shoes.

"Damn, hey you! Stop!"

But as he turned toward her, she moved around and was on her way.

At last, it loomed ahead. It was a beautiful chapel. Used formerly by the Count of Flanders, it was said the very cloth held in such high esteem there had the blood of Christ on it. It would have been quick of her to forget why she was there, as it was such an architecturally inspirational small chapel. But as her steps moved on, her heart began to beat like it had the morning after he had given up his room in Venice and then stole that infamous kiss from her in the breakfast room of the *Pensione*.

"I bet I know where your thoughts were and wonder if this is the most appropriate place to have them?"

She spun around so fast she had to grab his lapels to keep from falling down at his shoes. "Well, it's not entirely improper." Her heels went up as her toes lifted.

"Really. I don't believe you." His hands moved to hers, holding them tightly.

"Well, it is, of course, all your fault."

He leaned closer, moving her toward an alcove away from the few eyes there who were not out watching the race. "Of course, but why?"

"You caused my heart to race wildly back in Italy. Now again. I happened to just learn where you are. I came to find you as fast as I could."

"You must be wrong. You just exerted yourself, that's all." His eyes were so dark, and a dangerously handsome smirk creased the sides of his mouth as he leaned down and kissed her gently.

She softly moaned into his mouth as their tongues touched. He pulled back slightly and then placed a gentle kiss on the curve of her lusciously warm skin.

"If you let go of me now, I will slither down to my boots." Her breath was shallow. Words hardly heard.

"I'll always be here to help you. Carry you. Always."

They stood, eyes locked, as he kissed her again. This time was not so gentle or quick.

"Ah, hum."

No response.

"Ah, hum. I assume you two are here to ask me to write up and post bands of marriage for your upcoming nuptials?"

They pulled apart, smiling.

"Father G! Can we get back to you on that? Oh, and it's darn good to see you again." Adam shook his hand.

"Still not ready, are you two? I would have thought this last big one would have sealed the deal. Well, you know how to shut the door on your way out and where I am when you are ready."

He disappeared into the sacristy.

"I need some time alone with just you. What about we sneak to the cottage and hide out there for a few days?" He had just closed the outside church door and was taking her hand in his.

"I checked my schedule and I'm free for at least a week." They continued along the path, both spotting that exact location where once, not that long ago, they had made love and nearly ruined the baker's new pie concoction.

"We have memories all over the globe, Adam. But I want to make sure we have more here than anywhere else. I don't know how you could have known what was going on back with Rano and not come and dragged me away. Then flogged me."

"You have to keep it in perspective. Someday that role may be reversed. We can't always remember every bit of all our lives until it's time. Or it would simply be too easy. I did know you and he were in love. But it was a different one than what we have."

"Yes. Before we get there, do you have any questions about it, him or me? I want to get that right out of the way now. It seems some of my memory of that era is quickly fading."

"Nope, I'm good. Anything you want to ask me?"

She shrugged, and then gave into the jabber inside her mind. "Yes and no." Her eyes remained steady with his as they continued to walk along. But she refused to ask the question burning on her tongue.

He spun her around to face him. "Then I will answer you so we can put all of this to rest forever more. One. Do you need to know more?"

She giggled and then laughed out loud, nearly doubling over.

"That's funny?"

"You have a will of iron then, Lord Griffin. Because I saw many lovely women all around you. Must have been a few broken hearts when you disappeared."

He kept them moving right along now inside the cottage and shoved a boot against the door, closing it with a thud. "I bathed at the pools on my own after that. Although I visited their houses a few times later, it was to gather up some errant soldiers and get them back to camp in one piece. That was not my agenda on this passage. As I found out after. And may I add, that a certain beautiful erotic dancer stole my heart. Teased me relentlessly. Then simply disregarded my existence and vanished off with another?"

She blushed sweetly as he swept her up into his arms and placed a solid kiss on her partially parted lips. "I fully expect you will remember how to do that here. Right?"

They both inhaled the sweetness around them.

"Smell that? Fresh pie, bread, and meats. I think someone else knew of our arrival today and planned. We have to thank Mrs. H at some point."

"So, what was it then? I have a feeling you need to tell me one more thing. Something you have deliberately not told me since we arrived in Belgium."

"Damn you are so perceptive," he laughed, smoothing both hands up her ass as they headed up the stairs.

"Well?" They were now in her room, both of them releasing each other momentarily from a locked gaze to look at the bed.

"Fine. I see no other way around this except to tell you straight up front that Rano and I were brothers. Twins, separated at birth because our mother thought I may not live. She did not wish to give a sickly child to her husband as the heir apparent first born."

"But you two must have been fraternal then, right? As you were not identical. Wow, now that I think of it, you would pass for brothers."

"Correct on both. We shared the same indent on the back of our necks."

"I know that now. But never put the two together for some damn reason. What happened?"

"She gave me up to a nice settled pair in a neighboring village."

"Semite village?"

"You are smart. Yes. I was raised by them. I did not know I was to be reunited with my brother until I met you and we started out on this long journey from Venice back to here. Several times. You see, part of the reason why he could not settle his soul was his love for you. Also, his love of me. He had found out later in life about me and worked tirelessly behind the scenes so no one would know, to make sure we met—even going so far as to fight me himself in battle knowing I would be saved by our healer. You. But that was not all. Apparently our meeting there was always preempted by your choice to change the ending, so to speak, so I was never allowed to know. I am not telling you this to hurt you. But to help you realize how all our past actions can really cause a dissatisfying turn of events to occur in our futures."

"Wow. This is a lot more than I realized. I truly am so sorry. I hope it is all finally settled. I truly think it is. Believe me, I will keep this in the back of my mind. To make sure I really think about my actions before moving forward."

"I know you will. Until he is removed from your memory for good, you may still go through some strange feelings. Now I understand the voice that I heard from time to time. It was him. He affected you in an entirely different way."

"I'm sure we can agree that's a good thing."

They both smiled.

"He would somehow speak to me at times and make sure that we stayed on track in getting you and the jewels back to the craftsman and he reunited with it. He needed it all in place to rest in peace. You letting him go, the sword intact and seeing me one more time. I did not actually figure out it was my brother guiding us back in time through it all until he approached me in the encampment and told me everything."

They had crawled in bed naked, each on their side facing one another. "Adam I know it was me trying to save Rano. That I had pried the jewels off the sword as some kind of a remembrance and took them. That was eye-awakening to know it was me that was making us all keep repeating the same scenarios over and over again. The strangest part was that I never remembered meeting you until it was over and it started again."

"Yes, you have been playing with a lot of people's lives for a very long, long time, Sam, including ours."

"What happens now? We are both here. I have not been given a choice to return to my modern Exeter. What happens next?"

"Your original time is now. I don't think it all has settled in with you yet."

"I don't quite understand."

"Love, you dragged your heels in letting go of things and people, that's all. You made the choice long ago to stay here. But then you got confused and left. Over time you moved on to 2015 England and for some strange reason, those up there permitted you to remain for a while. That's the best explanation I have."

"As long as I don't do that all again, all will be well in the world?"

"Yes. That's your final step or stop. You already completed half of it by not taking the jewels off the sword and keeping them. The other part was you believing in being here. In other words, don't get restless. If you do, it will reverse what was done and lots of people, including me, will be quite angry with you."

She settled back on the pillow. "So how can we make sure I don't get restless? What can we do that we've never done before to ensure I always return here? Can I just go back and get my bike and ride it in secrecy?"

He slid on top of her. "You could do that. I will go with you to make sure you come back, mistress."

"Can we go in a few days? I need to make sure I have a list of what I want to bring so I don't have any reasons at all."

"I have another idea to throw into the mix. This will ensure we've done something that we never did before."

"What is it?"

He smiled. It was the most touching emotion that she would ever know. In this lifetime. That itself was different.

"Will you be my wife?"

She wove her hands up into his hair, feeling that notch once again. "Yes. I will. The sooner the better, please, and Adam?"

"Yes, love, I know. It's time to stop talking."

Chapter Thirteen

"Did you see the look on Mrs. H when she caught sight of my bike at the cottage?"

He laughed, pulling her tightly into his arms. "How do you like your wedding present? You are causing quite a stir all around the village. The paper wants to do a story on you."

She laughed, running her hand over the leather seat of the Velocipede, a very special ladies' bike he had imported from New York City. It was the height of fashion for women's two-wheeled transportation.

"Oh, I love it. Wait until I create ladies' pants and ride with those. It could launch a new style of clothing and make us rich before the rest of the world catches up years later."

He shook his head. "That's the last of your things from the cottage. You know I'll miss not coming down here for our afternoon trysts. Are you sure you want to give it up?"

"Absolutely. For Clash and Anne, I'd do anything. I can't wait for their wedding. You like him, don't you? I hear he gives a fair shake at your loot in cards."

"A shark, that's what he is. Even Victor has conceded that he's outsmarted us on more than one game. He fits in with our type. I'm glad you are happy giving up this place to them."

"Well, that's it then. Shall we?"

"Yeah, I also had one other thing done. The statue of Isis has been moved to our western garden. I thought you may like to still visit her. It is quite nice when the sun sets. She really does light up. I think she'd miss you not coming around."

She leaned over, kissing him while never missing a step wheeling the bike out. "I like that you had a shed built for this right outside the back. Being spoiled by you works for me."

He took the bike from her and kept going. "Well, we agreed as long as I keep you occupied and happy you won't get bored and go away." His voice was light, holding no uncertainty. Finally, it seemed they both were beginning to relax into this new marriage, believing it really was over.

"One area we certainly have diversity in is our sex life. I should be all set. That and the bike rides, of course."

He swatted her on the ass as he closed the shed door, eyeing the other bike in there from her Exeter cottage. She was still adamantly using it on the sly, even though the tires were small for the dirt-packed roads. Sliding the lock in place, he instantly felt the mood swing before she even opened her mouth.

"I'm a bit anxious to go to sleep tonight, Adam. It is six months to the night and the Tinker and the Sage both said all will be decided on within this timeline."

He knew.

"So you can wake up tomorrow and be assured that this is all real. That you were not transported back to 2015 England and start this all over again. I know. I have taken it upon myself to have Mrs. H serve us out on the patio. Winter is nearly upon us and it will be colder soon. I suggest we eat early then call it a night. I admit I feel the same. I want to wake up tomorrow and know you are still here. I'm sorely tempted to chain myself to your body. I should have taken that extra duct tape from your cottage before we returned here. That stuff would work for sure. I've never seen anything like it."

Hand in hand they went together to eat, both keenly noticing that even Mrs. H seemed unusually quiet this evening as she brought their dinner and left them to converse privately. Moving her foot out of a pump, Sam slid one silky foot up his leg as he eyed her suspiciously. Actually, a bit on the lusty side was more like it.

Mrs. H reappeared. "I'll just clear this off and you two can sit back and relax."

"Mrs. H, that was fantastic as always. Would you like to take a chair and have a nightcap with us? A bit of a catch-up?"

She shook her head "No, I'm ready to call it a night. Albeit an early one. Everyone has taken off already. Seems there are a lot of anxious people across the land. Good night to you both."

They both watched her leave.

"She thinks so too?"

"Yeah, we all are wanting this night over."

"What if it's the wrong one and it is actually tomorrow?"

"Can't be. It's on the calendar. We all cross-checked each other to make sure. Besides, that gypsy woman's readings have all been spot on, remember? Considering how much of what she said has come true. Like all of it. We can't just stop believing her at this juncture."

"Of course, you are right. Okay." She rose, sliding her hand over his shoulder and ruffling his hair. "You going to stay and smoke?"

He nodded, taking it out of his inside jacket pocket and lighting it up. "I won't be long." He watched her go, knowing the last time he saw this much anxiety in her, they were in the car on the way out of Mecca.

***

She went up through the main stairway, slowly, keeping a hand gripped tightly on the brass rail until she reached the third landing. Apprehension filled her entire body. Stopping, she leaned against the wall, glancing up at two of Adam's ancient ancestors and sensing they were anxious too.

"Okay, let's do this." She spoke directly to them. "It's now or never."

The long walk down their hall toward the double-wide suite doors seemed to take an eternity. Anxious as all hell would be an understatement. She stopped, gazing lovingly up at their newly painted wedding picture just before entering their suite.

"I love you, Adam," she whispered. Slowly pushing down on the handle, she entered, closing the door behind her. Undressing, she washed up, slid on her silk robe, and opened the balcony doors to step out where the sun had set. The last of its glow shone on the top of Isis.

The wind rustled her robe, untying it, but she did not notice. Nor the chill that wove up her spine. She closed her eyes and leaned slightly back, the robe billowing in the wind as his hands slid up her thighs, cupping her breasts, pinching both puckered peaks.

Sam released a moan into the night sky.

When his lips touched hers, she knew it was different.

"You are here."

"Yes, I saw this brazen woman exposing her luscious skin, like an angel, high up on my balcony and had to come quickly before she disappeared." He turned her into his arms and kissed her with torturing passion as she felt him against her thighs.

"You are naked."

"Absolutely. I could not come out here with such intention and not be. Being the goddess that you are, you may have turned your nose up at me."

"I thought you were a dream and he had returned. Ironically, your voices are so much alike."

"Nope. I am your barrier now. He will not get to you, nor would he try. He made me the promise that when you finally did this right, that throughout all the rest of our time, I would be the one. He gave me his word."

"Oh, how blessed I am to have the love of two great men."

He picked her up and slid her down on him as the robe fought fiercely to be released. She raised her arms and it released up and off, blowing out into the sky. He sat on the balcony bench as she arched back, taking him in deeper.

"You own me."

She had heard him say those words as well.

"No, I do not."

Their breathing was heavy as the raven passed by, adding his comments.

"Yes, you do."

He plunged so deep into her their release brought a moan from their lips. As the kiss deepened, so did their shared release.

He pushed hair back from her face, tucking it behind both ears while her nails dug into his back. "You are going to leave scars, woman."

She smiled. "Take us to our bed, husband."

It was the first time she'd said that. To him, no words could mean more except when she said she loved him.

"As you command, mistress."

"Oh, I shall always love that word."

"I know you will. But you are so much more than that. You are the trifecta. My wife, mistress, and soul mate."

"Adam, I love you so. Please hold me tight all the rest of this night until the sun rises into tomorrow's sky. I cannot help it. I still have doubts."

He allowed no distance between them as he covered them with the sheets and blankets. "I'm right here."

She tried so hard to stay awake, chattering away. But even he could not, Sam noticed, as he dozed off. But she did remain stuck to him like glue throughout the night.

***

Then the dream started.

She tossed and turned and was in and out of his arms. He felt her restlessness and pulled her back against him. Finally, she settled something inside those dreams and slept again.

Damn. Was this right?

As the raven flew by along with a few of his friends and the sun shone, he turned over. Her spot was warm but vacant. Jumping up, he could not see the balcony. Yet, with each purposeful step his heart was moving further and further into his throat.

He stopped, stepping out onto the balcony and grabbed her tightly into his arms. She was here.

"You thought so as well, for just a second, didn't you?" Her smile was warm and inviting.

"Did you do that to me on purpose? You wench."

"I like the trifecta. There is no more room to add another."

"And smartass as well."

"Yes, and this smartass is going to be harassing you for a very, very long time." She turned and kissed him, and then flexed out over the balcony. "Look over there. I could not stop laughing earlier. Surprised I did not wake you."

"What?" He looked out over the west garden and could not believe his eyes. Her robe had not only taken flight last night, but it was draped around Isis.

"Shall we leave it there?"

"Hell no. I want it back here with you. That is the most bizarre thing I've ever seen."

"It was your brother. You two still work in cahoots. He removed it and you plundered. You damn thieving men."

He burst out laughing. "Who knows, you could be right. But, all the same, I'm going to throw on some trousers and boots and run down there and get it before anyone else sees it and wonders who the hell it belongs to.

Then, we have to start to explain. Or in your case, create such a story no one will believe a word either way." He turned, dressed and dashed out in a flash.

She watched his strong form run down the path and untie the robe. Then he threw his hands up in the air in mock victory, looked around, and ran back up the path into the house. He was not even breathless as he came into the room and out onto the balcony to show off his prize.

***

"Okay, where the hell are you?"

Silence.

He turned into the room and saw her. How the hell could anyone do that? She was in what would be described as a position straight out of the ancient Asian Kama Sutra. "Is that comfortable? How the hell are you holding that position?"

"Stretching. In the future years, I did a lot of yoga. I remember the poses. Want to come on over and see what happens?"

He threw the robe toward one of the chairs, but it missed and slid to the carpet. "Yup, sign me up."

She maneuvered him inside of her as his roaming hands halted. The heat quickly engulfed them both as an intense tremble followed.

"Lord Griffin, I like that. I think you should come into the future to learn yoga."

He laughed, sliding a hand up her curvy waist to cup a firm breast. "Perhaps a trip to the future, yes. But to a bookstore to get a copy of those poses in print."

They both laughed harder.

"I think a while back I made mention of our meeting again in our next life. Instead of doing passages we just get married young, have half a dozen kids and a very normal, British life. What do you think?"

"Did that come out again because of what I did?"

"It sure did. It is not just what you did, it's wow,

what you did. If you owned a brothel and taught all your women that move, men would be lined up for miles to get in and would pay any sum to stay."

She smiled warmly. "I have a few others to try out on you. We don't need that book."

"Oh, I like this being married stuff."

"Like I've said all along, we did not have to marry to have this. But now that I am married, I'd not give it up for anything."

"I know you are happy. I feel it."

She leaned in, kissing him. "Yes, I really am. Thank you."

He tugged her down. "Unfortunately, I am completely wiped out. So, unless you have some secret Chinese medicine tucked someplace in your herbal bags, healer, I need to have food and drink to sustain me. I doubt I can even rise from the bed and get dressed, I am so expended."

She grinned like an alley cat. "I'm hungry too. I wish you had a bike as well so we could ride together. Set a new trend. Start tails a wagging and all. Then all the aristocrats that stick their noses up at us will want to copy."

They both rose and dressed and then headed out of the room to eat while chatting away.

"I did. I ordered two of the ladies' bikes and the gypsy's son is rearranging it for my size. You know, he's quite resourceful with designing. While I was there, he showed me some of his ideas. I am going to sponsor him to full University in this upcoming winter session at Oxford. I had to pull in some markers to get him accepted, but he's going. I could not let his talent go to waste. Not like he was not using some of it on the road, but now he can look at some options for a future if he chooses to."

"Oh, Adam, that is fantastic."

"They are going to stay the winter and make sure he's comfortable before moving on."

"Can't they stay longer? I like spending time with her."

"I know you do. It did not take much to persuade her. This will be a first. Her youngsters are going to go to school. But she does not want to give up their caravan. I'll make sure they are all comfortable. She's done a lot for us."

"As long as she feels like she's contributing. You know how they abhor charity."

"Her son is going to work while in classes. I have arranged it with an associate's agency. He can start from the ground up learning about design properly. He will earn a modest wage and have to work his ass off. But he was keen enough when we talked about it in length. He has potential. I'm just giving him a hand up, that's all."

"I always said it. You are a good bloke, Lord Griffin."

He laughed, reaching for her hand. They entered the breakfast room but then halted.

"What's all this? Are we expecting company?"

Indeed, they were.

Mrs. H came in with Anne, Clash, Victor, her sister-in-law, the kids, the gypsy, her kids as well as her husband and Father G.

"Mrs. H?"

"It's time to celebrate, Master Griffin. We made it. All our lives are going to get a bit easier now that the mistress has settled in."

Father G took Sam by the arm, bringing her over to sit beside him and Victor. "She means you are..."

"Oh, Father, I know what she means. I more than you all am overjoyed at still being here this morning."

"So perhaps I won't see you two so much on the back path heading behind the cottage now that you are properly married?"

Sam blushed as Adam grinned. "Now, Father, you

know how we both like to take in a bit of fresh air. This English weather is more temperamental than the spirited woman I met long ago in Venice."

"Stop it. Don't speak around me." She eyed the children, grateful they were having a hard time following the adult bantering. Father G seemed to read her mind and silently agreed, nodding at her. "If I may steer this conversation, which I started, back to a more serious note. You did it, Sam, finally."

She grinned, lifting her juice glass. "With a lot of help from all of you and a few others around the globe. This is to us all."

THE END... Perhaps.

About Sandra Waine

Sandra Waine currently resides in central New Hampshire with her cat, Irene. Along with writing, she also enjoys cycling, hiking, traveling and photography. As well, she is a Level 2 Usui Reiki Practitioner.

Social Media Links:

Author website: www.sandrawaine.com

Facebook:
https://www.facebook.com/profile.php?id=100000005071
04

Twitter: https://twitter.com/@slwaine777

If you enjoyed this story, check out these other Solstice Publishing books by Sandra Waine:

Passages A Trilogy Book 1 Touch Me From Afar
It only took twenty-four hours for Samantha Arnesen's world to change drastically and there was no logical explanation for it. Divorced, forty and needing a complete change, she ditched a logical, safe world back in England and took off exploring other parts of Europe.

A rather embarrassing circumstance in Venice propels Sam into a bold interaction with a handsome stranger. Had she left things alone her safe little life would have continued. But it was not her destiny. A passionate kiss transcends her right into his world of 1865.

Was it irrational, destiny, or a bump on the head?

With no apparent possibility of returning back, it all simply starts to unravel.

https://bookgoodies.com/a/B01N9PXR7N

Passages A Trilogy Book 2 What Have You Unearthed?

As book two continues, Sam finds herself thrust into an uprising in modern day Egypt with bold, daring cameraman, Derek Clash. They team up brilliantly. But it's clear he has an agenda that extends beyond just helping her. Somehow, he's entangled with more than one person from her Victorian past.

With assistance from strange outside sources, a small group

of ex-military men turned mercenary and the good sisters of a small leper monastery, Sam and Derek soon discover how intense their connection really is.

Separately, Adam moves on a different path and passages. But along the way, he realizes how important Sam has become to him. Finally, they intertwine on a journey that brings them both to internal discoveries that are far beyond anything a great imagination could ever conjure.

But her past won't lay silent. In fact, it's drawing her closer and closer to an event that will take them both down the dark tunnel of their soul's journey. Back in time to a powerful Egyptian dynasty. Their future, their love, and the existence of others hinge on how they both act and react during this period.

https://bookgoodies.com/a/B06XXPJB4R